A **DARK** TALE FROM COTTONWOOD GROVE

A **DARK** TALE FROM COTTONWOOD GROVE

MAHFUD IKHWAN

Translated by Annie Tucker

SPEAKING TIGER

SPEAKING TIGER BOOKS
125A, Ground Floor, Shahpur Jat
New Delhi – 110049

First published in Bahasa Indonesia as
Dawuk: Kisah Kelabu Dari Rumbuk Randu by Marjin Kiri 2017
First published in English by Speaking Tiger Books 2024

ISBN: 978-93-5447-761-4
eISBN: 978-93-5447-892-5

10 9 8 7 6 5 4 3 2 1

Typeset in Adobe Garamond Pro by SÜRYA, New Delhi
Printed at Shree Maitrey Printech Pvt. Ltd., Noida

Contents

Morning Coffee

'JUST A FEW hours ago, within shooting distance from here, was the most vicious attack since the Japanese stormed Kawak Boarding School, and the place is this quiet? Not even one person is talking about it? Bah!'

He charged into the small open-air cafe, a sarong draped over his head, and slapped both palms down on the table, like a famous *gendang* drummer: imperious and commanding attention. Two empty cups sitting on the table hopped up from their saucers.

'No, nobody's talking about it,' he repeated, shaking his head. 'Unbelievable!'

He plunked down onto the long bench like a cranky child, then stamped his agitated feet on the dirt floor. In a pair of flip-flops, one worn clean through at the heel and the other with a string of raffia replacing its plastic thong, those feet were as dusty and dirty as a charcoal burner who hadn't yet had the chance to clean himself up after a hard day's work.

'All you think about is those little hunks of wood!' he barked at the chess players beside him. 'As if you were government loggers!' They remained focused on their game. One of them glared over, to signal his annoyance, then returned to his whittled pawns. The man's arrival was being more or less ignored.

'The only thing you all care about is the election outcome for village head in Tegal Londo! Damn you!' This rebuke seemed addressed to everyone in the coffee *warung*. 'If Haji Jarkasi wins, is he going to foot the bill to send you all to Mecca? Or if it turns out Secretary Wibowo will be the next village head, will he appoint you all to his advisory committee?' His grumbling ascended into a shout: 'Coffee!'

The reply he was waiting for didn't come. 'Yoo-hoo, Siti! Coffee!' Now, he was howling.

'You don't have to shout!' said a woman from the kitchen. 'We're in a *warung*, not the middle of the forest!'

The man with the sarong draped over his head like a lady's headscarf smiled at that testy reply.

'You want it sweet or black?' came a yell.

'The usual!'

A moment later, a middle-aged woman appeared, her eyebrows furrowed as if a bad dream had just woken her from a deep sleep. She practically threw the tarnished white cup down onto the table. Thick black liquid splattered out from under its lid set askew, dripped down through its cracked handle, then slowly puddled in its stained saucer. Anyone looking at this overflow could tell the coffee was only partially brewed and watered down. It had almost certainly been poured carelessly, stirred lazily, if at all and—as just clearly demonstrated—served with resentment.

'When will you pay your tab, huh?' the server snapped. 'I'm not some rich Mrs So-and-So who's sitting on a pile of money. If I don't get paid, I'll go out of business!'

Nonchalant, his head still covered, the man grabbed the cracked handle, poured the cup's remaining contents into the saucer until that too almost overflowed, blew on it three times, lifted it to his mouth and took a hearty swallow. The loud gulps emanating from his throat seemed meant as an insult.

'I'll pay you everything I owe! Start totalling it now, and my son will send it next month. I'll pay interest, too; if you insist, that's fine.' He licked his lips and unkempt grey moustache as if he didn't want to miss even one tepid drop. 'Ah, you didn't even boil the water, did you?'

'That's enough out of you!' As the woman walked back through the doorway into the kitchen, she muttered, 'You old loudmouth, you're lucky I didn't use water scooped straight from the tub. Or maybe next time you'd like it mixed with bitter herbs?'

Pretending not to hear her, he ran his thumb over his mouth and moustache and then licked it.

'You all don't know about the attack?' he asked again, looking around. The coffee had restored his initial disbelief. 'Or you could call it a beating, whichever you prefer.' Forsaking the chess players, who were unmoved by his jabber, he now scooched down the bench, aiming himself at a group of card players in another corner and those gathered around them, watching.

He slid the sarong down from his head to his shoulders, stood up, took the half-empty cup, approached the huddle and sat down again, just a little too eager and a little too close. He made some gestures to call attention to himself, but no one seemed to pick up on his cues. Jeers and laughter erupted from the centre of the group—but in reaction to a ridiculous move by one of the players, not his approach. Still, he wouldn't give up that easily.

'I thought, after the Japanese captured Mat Modar and after the district military commander picked up two members of Udeng Ireng in Cucukan Village for their improper practice of the faith, and then the whole line-up in 1965, there wouldn't be any more of these incidents. But it turns out…' he shook his head, with a deeply pained expression, 'People still do such things.' He shook his head again. 'How could it be that for just one man they came swarming, like a crowd from the mosque after Friday prayers?'

He raised his cup to his lips again, sipping his coffee slowly and then pausing, as if he were a kung-fu master in an old silent film. Maybe he was hoping that one or two guys would look at him with curiosity and then, growing impatient, ask a question. But after he had lowered his coffee cup, which was now probably down to the dregs, those damned cards still remained the focus of attention—everyone laughed again as someone drew a ten and then slammed it down. He looked left and right, then started fidgeting around in the pockets of his shorts. It was easy to guess he wanted a cigarette, but even though everyone was caught up in the game, no one had left their pack forgotten on the table.

'Sure, of course, in a big crowd like that, they could

easily trounce a poor young man who had already lost the will to live. No doubt that must have been how the Japanese bastards got Mat Modar. Binding his hands, whipping him, and dragging him the whole length of Kawak Bridge before shooting him in the middle of the forest—or at least, that's how the story goes. But of course, everything can be set right with cooperation. *Gotong-royong*. That's what they taught us in school, right, during our Pancasila lessons? The principles of state ideology must govern everything we say and do, isn't that true? So even murder requires "unity and community"!'

A fleck of foam appeared at the left corner of his mouth. His coffee was obviously finished now, but still, no one tilted an ear in his direction. They didn't even pretend to acknowledge him.

He looked as though he were beginning to surrender. He began to edge away unobtrusively, moving slowly as if he didn't want anyone to notice his departure—an incompetent huckster making an embarrassing exit. The *warung* owner wouldn't have to be goaded into scolding him anymore that morning because he passed right by her, bringing his umpteenth unpaid tab with him. He hooded the edge of his sarong back over his head, completing his shamefaced retreat.

'Ah, you're full of it, 'To!'

The reproach stopped him in his tracks.

'To? So this was Warto? The notorious Warto, known in all the food and coffee stalls around here? I'd frequented lots of spots during my work for a small-time newspaper, and I'd heard all about him.

Someone else quickly chimed in, 'Is it so hard to speak the truth every once in a while, 'Plung?'

It had to be.

Plung was a nickname that came from the local word *kemplung*, which meant bullshit. This was the man: Warto Kemplung. Warto the Bullshitter—or, since his first name 'Warto' could mean 'news', you could also just call him 'Fake News'.

I'd heard he got the nickname after loudly proclaiming that, while off seeking his fortune in Malaysia, he had become friends with a high-ranking Malaysian official Indonesians would later come to know as Leader of the Opposition, Anwar Ibrahim. Based on the rumours and gossip that spread throughout the coffee stalls and cafes around here, this tall tale that earned him the name Kemplung could be summarized as follows:

Years ago, Warto and some other migrant workers he knew were renovating the house of a royal official; they learned that the house belonged to Anwar Ibrahim, who at that time was the Minister of Education; as they worked, Warto, who talked a lot, told his friends a story about Mat Modar, a mysterious local figure from the war for independence whom he mentioned from time to time; after work his friends went home, but the homeowner invited him to stay and chat; apparently, Anwar Ibrahim had overheard the story about Mat Modar and wanted to know more about him and hear more of Warto's stories; through these regular after-work story sessions, the two eventually grew close; their friendship was demonstrated, according to Warto's account, by Anwar asking his kids to call Warto

'Uncle', giving Warto his private phone number, and telling him not to hesitate to contact him at any time should he ever need anything; their good relationship lasted after Anwar's home improvements were finished; and because of that good relationship—and Anwar's personal phone number—Warto claimed he had never been bothered by the Royal Malaysia Police, even though his documents were not always in order; he only ran into trouble, and was eventually put in jail and deported, after Anwar was accused of sodomy and corruption and was suspended from his position as Deputy Prime Minister; but prison actually only made the friendship between Warto and Anwar grow stronger, since fate reunited them in the same cell in the Buloh River Prison in Selangor, and because of that they remained close friends to this day.

Of course, no one believed that story. Warto had been known as Warto Kemplung ever since, and everyone still considers him full of it.

'According to what I heard,' one sceptic in the crowd said, 'a *kyai* from Lasem or somewhere injured that guy in a duel, man-to-man. Because the legal system didn't punish him for his crimes as it should have, the people had to uphold justice themselves. So, they threw him into the fire, burning him alive inside that ramshackle hut where he used to live with his wife.'

'After he surrendered his trusty weapon and the amulet around his neck to his father-in-law, isn't that right?' sneered Warto, barely looking over in the man's direction. He held that position for a moment, letting his words sink in. 'Isn't that right?' It was a question he seemed sure only he himself could answer.

'Well, yes…isn't that right?' the sceptic echoed back at him, this time sounding a little uncertain.

This was the kind of question Warto adored, the tone of doubt he had been yearning for, just as the cold drink seller watches for signs of thirst and the balloon peddler dreams of clamouring children. He swiftly turned his back for a moment to take the sarong down off his head again and tie it around his waist in the usual way so that it covered his threadbare drawstring shorts and his bare calves, blackened with soot and dust. He approached the questioner with a sly and victorious grin, straightaway snatching the pack of cigarettes and lighter from his hand. Warto—Warto Kemplung, to be exact—pinched two cigarettes from that poor sucker whose own curiosity had gotten the better of him, tucked one behind his ear, and in the same fluid motion, slipped the other between his lips and lit it.

'They bragged about his defeat, about how he surrendered his weapon and the amulet, about the fire, and yet they never once mentioned the assault—and you can bet they aren't going to say anything about the beam of white light that came shooting out from the flames!' Warto Kemplung spoke with a know-it-all's self-assurance.

'White light?'

Warto Kemplung grinned, showing his brownish-yellow teeth, which were perhaps the result of cigarettes, coffee, and a decades-long aversion to toothbrushes.

'Coffee! Another! The usual!' he shouted, radiant, like a small-time gambler who has just bankrupted his bookie. I settled into my seat. I was ready to hear a tale from the infamous Warto Kemplung, and I had a feeling this was going to be good.

The Man with the Cleft Lip

THE STORY I'M about to tell you didn't happen so very long ago. The dark, bloody chain of events came to pass just after Golkar beat the United Development Party in a landslide for the first time in this district, two election cycles ago, right when the new village headman took office. But because I know what kind of people you are—wretched creatures with the memories of gourami fish—let us begin with the most recent events.

A little over a month ago, on an ordinary weekend afternoon when people didn't expect much of anything to happen, he appeared from around a bend in the road at the northernmost border of Cottonwood Grove, his wife's village, after he had disappeared and been gone for fifteen years. His arrival was quite a surprise, maybe because, as all the news about him had long ago subsided like a dying wind, most people had thought—and hoped—that he was dead. Indeed, he should have been dead. Or maybe it was because no one in that village imagined he would ever return. Surely no one wanted him to return.

Not many knew his true history, but everyone knew he

was dangerous. When he appeared around that far bend in the road at dusk, with nothing but the clothes on his back and a mysterious lumpy bundle stuffed inside a plastic Mydin Malaysia grocery bag, no one even attempted to greet him. Or maybe it's more accurate to say everyone acted as though they didn't recognize him.

He had changed since his disappearance—he had gone from just ugly to truly hideous, you'll understand what I mean later—but of course, he knew he'd be hard to forget; he must certainly have realized that at least a few folks remembered him and were pretending not to. That was no problem for him, though; he was happy to be left alone, just as he had left others alone his whole life. He was a feral and reclusive child who had grown into a withdrawn man who practically loathed the presence of others, so he certainly hadn't returned from his long journey in search of a warm welcome. I'm sure he missed his wife and he wanted to be with her, nothing more.

He had lived through this before, after all: on the seventh evening after the first incident, before he left town for the second time, he had stumbled through town, battered, bruised, and bleeding, and the people had just stared, if not hastened to shut their windows and lock their doors. So, it was fine with him when he arrived at the house where he had once lived with his wife, which was now dilapidated from neglect, that not one of his neighbours extended words of greeting or disturbed him with friendly small talk. They didn't even taunt him as they had in his boyhood.

Ah, well, he didn't even really have neighbours. There

were four garden plots and two more unkempt fields, choked with shrubs and clusters of banana trees, between the next house and the one he returned to and soon began to repair. He was happy when, very early the following morning, the people who passed by on their way into the forest, puzzled by the cracks and thuds of wood and bamboo being split and snapped, quickly returned to their own business once they realized, from a distance, who they saw in the ruins. And he felt calmer when no one interrupted him, let alone came to comfort him, as he tried with all his might to drown out his sobs, lamentations, and piteous yearning moans for his wife with the blasting hum of the sander and the choked whine of the blunt chainsaw he was using for repairs. The following afternoon, when he went to his wife's grave on the far side of the village, and people stepped aside as if to give him as wide as possible a path to walk by, he felt like they were doing him a favour. It was the five thousandth day after his wife's death.

At night, he could sink into his solitude, alone with the old Indian songs he used to listen to with his wife, and no one complained about the noise. (Who knows what he used to play them: an old tape recorder that had been left behind, or a new model player he had brought home with him?) He remained impassive as people kept their distance when he joined the congregation to pray. He didn't take it to heart when, at the time of greeting, people extended their hands in every other direction but his.

He basically just accepted them all: those who knew him but pretended not to, those reluctant to greet him and those who kept their distance. The problem came from the children, who didn't know him—who certainly hadn't even been born at the time of the incident—but who couldn't contain their amazement at the strange man who had suddenly appeared at their mosque.

At first, they just whispered about the prayers he was reciting, which didn't match up with any verse their religious teachers had ever told them to memorize and sounded even stranger coming out of such a peculiar mouth and nose. It's not a normal prayer, one of them said, it's not Arabic. Maybe it's Bawean, ventured another. A third guessed it could be Madurese, mixed with some other language they speak over in Sumatra. Or maybe it's Dayak, still another said.

Then, after he left, their gossip grew bolder. 'What a weird-looking nose, huh?' a child began.

His friend agreed, adding that it wasn't just his nose that was weird but his mouth too. Another brazen friend painted a more vivid picture: his nose was half caved in and his lip was ripped, or maybe it would be more accurate to say, cleft. 'It's not weird,' he declared, 'it's scary!'

After discussing it for a while, the kids made some hypotheses. Maybe he had a drunken accident after too much palm wine. Well, perhaps he had been drunk, but that wasn't how his face got like that. So how did it happen? It could be that he was intoxicated, and then he drove, and then he hit someone with his motorbike, and then that person died, and then a mob attacked him.

The guesses went further. With such a scary face, one kid imagined that that strange man hadn't been in an accident, hadn't been beaten up but…

'But…'

He didn't dare continue with his theory, and his friends who could guess what he would say didn't dare chime in. It wasn't because they were afraid they were wrong—it was because, with some scared little yelps, they were afraid they were right.

But don't think the kids stopped there. When the man reappeared at the mosque, the whispers started up again. The kids would scatter if he seemed to hear them and looked over in their direction. But they would gather again soon after, this time just a little bit farther away, and because as the days passed, their huddle got bigger, it wasn't just the man who noticed, but eventually their parents.

'Don't make so much noise!' That's what the grownups said at first.

'Don't make trouble!' came their second warning, a sign their children's behaviour was truly starting to get on their nerves. Then, when the fierce whispers reached an unruly crescendo, the parents finally asked: 'What's going on here?'

And that was the question the children had been waiting for. Now, with that question, they were granted permission to ask their parents about the man with the sunken-in nose, the cleft lip, and the strange way of saying his prayers. Once they had returned from the mosque, the questions filled their homes.

'Who is he, Dad?'

'Who is he, Mom?'

'Who is he, Sis?'

'Who is he, Grandpa?'

Of course, those questions didn't get immediate replies. The kids needed to entice and insist, and then, before they finally got their answers, they were forced to wait as whoever they had asked sat in silence for a moment, then drew in a long breath before finally uttering the name in a sombre half-whisper.

'Mat Dawuk…'

Mat Dawuk. Mat Dawuk. Two words the people of Cottonwood Grove could not utter without a shiver. And they weren't just trying to frighten their children—in all honesty, they themselves were terribly afraid, and they didn't want the kids to know how uncomfortable it made them to have those two words, that strange man's name, coming out of their mouths.

If those parents still discerned a bit of unsatisfied curiosity in their children's eyes, then with gentle persuasion, they would tell them to be quiet; it was enough now. If a firmer reprimand was needed, they would conclude with the threat: 'Or you'll be sorry!'

Yes, of course, it was like that; it was better that way. How could the parents tell their children—or how could the grandfathers and grandmothers say to their grandchildren, little innocent kids—the story of a man who had murdered his wife?

His wife and at least a few other people, to be exact.

Ina and Mat

'But you're not kids anymore, are you? So don't worry, I'll tell you all about it. And about the murder. But might I have another cigarette? Ah, that's it.'

As someone in the crowd offered Warto Kemplung a cigarette, I lit one of mine, thinking—murdered his wife? This seemed a bit much, but I admit I was drawn in. He took a long drag. 'Now, where were we?'

The murder, or what people were calling a murder, only happened a month after Inayatun—Inayatun, take note of that name because you're going to be hearing it quite often—returned home from Malaysia.

Just as with previous homecomings, her family hadn't exactly been looking forward to her return, and this time, it was quite embarrassing for them because she came home with Mat Dawuk and told her family and everyone else in Cottonwood Grove that they were married.

The people of Cottonwood Grove had grown accustomed to news of expedient marriages, elopements, marriages of convenience or whatever you all like to call it, after decades of sending their children or other family off to work in

Malaysia. But it was still difficult to accept Inayatun calling Mat Dawuk her husband. It's like this: you might carry a bushel of corn, a bundle of cassava, a sheaf of beans or a bunch of bananas home from the fields, but if you come home carrying a field rat and you call it a bunny rabbit, that's unacceptable. Insane.

Ina, as her father and mother called her, had been spoiled ever since she was a little girl. To borrow the title of a Rhoma Irama song, she was *The Village Prima Donna*. 'She was a flower in full bloom; everyone wanted to pluck her, to plant her heart deep inside their heart, to tend her blossom in their pot'…does anyone remember the rest?

She was a baby with big eyes, plump cheeks, light skin and an adorable little cooing mouth. Neighbours would fight over who got to hold her. Pregnant women, or women who were hoping to get pregnant, would look at her face and rub their bellies, wishing for a daughter like her. The postnatal health officers would beam as they lifted her onto the scale, seeing her as proof of their excellent work. She won the district's Independence Day Healthy Baby competition two years in a row. The marks on her medical records were perfect. The point is, out of all the families in Cottonwood Grove, she was the prime example of the success of the governmental program designed to improve the health of Indonesian mothers and children in the early stages of Suharto's third Five Year Plan. Don't believe me? You can go check the Cottonwood Grove social welfare archives, if they still exist.

Before she was a grown up, her admirers were no longer neighbours and health workers but the boys she knew. Ina was an early bloomer. Before she had entered her adolescence, her wide, innocent child eyes precociously narrowed into those of a seductress. Her breasts and hips grew much faster than the other young girls her age, and they stuck out farther. (This is where she got the nickname Ina Indomilk—yup, just like cans of sweet, condensed milk.) Even before the end of primary school, half of the boys her age, if they had been forced to answer, would have admitted to squeezing her breasts or grabbing her behind—and those who wouldn't have admitted it, of course, can't be counted. When she had just barely turned fourteen, it was rumoured she already had a baby in her belly, but a witch doctor in a faraway village gave her a special massage so that it came out long before it could grow to term.

Inayatun grew into an attractive young woman—men liked her, but she was a headache for her family. Her father, Imamudin (the people called him Pak Imam out of respect), was well known for his deep religious knowledge and had been a teacher in the village for many years. Her mother, Sulaikah, was an enthusiastic and admired prayer group leader. At all kinds of events, from Independence Day celebrations in the village hall to Mawlid celebrations at the mosque, to weddings or circumcisions at a neighbour's house, wherever there was seating for special guests, the family would always be invited to take the very front row. They, of course, had hoped for a pious daughter—not just for her own good in the hereafter, but also for the good of her family here in this world—but what could they do? What they got was a bad girl who was difficult to control and who did only what she wanted. Inayatun had a talent for prayer recitation, but she was just as gifted at seducing men. Melodious Arabic rolled off her tongue, but she was just as fluent when hurling insults and talking dirty.

It wasn't surprising that some people, especially the women who used to yearn for a daughter like her, now painted her out to be a disaster. They called her 'Ina-lillahi', Ina who belongs to Allah, of course while clutching their chests and shaking their heads. Before middle school was out, when the only boys in the throes of puberty not dreaming about stroking her cheek or kissing her lips were the ones who had already done it, mothers no longer wished they had a daughter like her. Those who had given their swelling stomachs little aspirational pats while gazing at Inayatun now stroked their bellies, murmuring protective chants and lullabies and asking for Allah's forgiveness.

Saying they wanted to improve their daughter's morals, but maybe at the same time hoping to get her out of the house and as far away as possible, Pak Imam planned to send Inayatun to a distant Islamic boarding school as soon as she finished middle school. But, maybe because she knew that this was her father's way of getting rid of her, or perhaps because she did want more freedom to enjoy men's praise, Inayatun instead asked permission to go even farther away. 'To make you happy, Father,' she said lightly.

'Where, then?' Pak Imam sighed.

Casually, she replied, 'Malaysia.'

'Why?' Pak Imam now roared. 'You want to go off and become a whore?'

'Who knows...' the girl said with a toothy grin.

Pak Imam indeed regretted his words, which, in retrospect, seemed more like a curse. After she left, Inayatun never sent money home like most who went to find work in Malaysia—in fact, it wasn't clear what kind of work she had found, if any. She wasn't contracted to a project, she wasn't doing factory work nor had she become a maid.

'She's probably selling milk!' That was the joke at the local coffee stall.

'It must be going cheap since it has no resale value,' someone else would chime in, always met with hearty laughter.

She rarely phoned or mailed a letter home. What reached the house more often were rumours, most of which did not sit well: she had eloped with someone, run away with someone's husband or ruined someone's life. Inayatun came home three times after her initial departure, and each time she brought a new husband or a new man she called husband. Mat Dawuk, so they say, was her fourth.

Coming home with different men all the time, that was embarrassing; but pairing up with Mat Dawuk and parading him in front of her parents was an outrage.

'Why don't you just throw shit on your mother's face!' her mother shrieked before fainting.

'How broken are you that you could do such a thing?' her father asked in disgust.

That was the question almost everyone had, and such a question was not unwarranted. Mat Dawuk's face was nearly as ugly as his name. He wasn't from Cottonwood Grove, but a ruinous family in Deep Well Village. I can tell you about it later, if I get the chance. Even so, everyone in Cottonwood Grove knew about him, or at least they knew this: he was the ugly, wild boy who had spent his childhood roaming about in their fields, gardens and graveyards.

It's hard to explain how ugly Mat Dawuk had been as a child, and it's just as difficult to explain how terrifying his face was as an adult. To make it easier, let's just put it this way: if he were your kid or your nephew, you wouldn't want to admit it.

His given name was good, even grand: Muhammad Dawud, which, of course, means beloved. But, because he had been dirty, rumpled, and uncared for as a child, the people of Cottonwood Grove mocked him by calling him 'dawuk', a local word they usually reserved for goats with grey coats. And so, he had become known as Mat Dawuk.

Worse than his face was his fate. Most people didn't want to associate with him, but his father hated him, not only because his son was deformed, but because he held Mat responsible for the loss of his wife, who died giving birth to him. Yes, that man—don't ask his name—was a wretched father who cared about nothing but the cocks he bred for fighting and the cheap whores he was always frequenting. If Mat Dawuk tried to approach, the man would wave him away, especially if he was busy with his roosters. If the boy called for him, he would get yelled at in reply, and if he pleaded for some pocket money, all he would get was a smack.

Before Mat Dawuk met Inayatun, perhaps only one other person in the world had ever loved or cared about him: his grandfather. Mbah Dulawi, as his grandfather was called, was the one who had given his deformed grandson such a good name. Sadly, his grandfather wasn't with him for very long. When Mat Dawuk was about five years old, Dulawi disappeared—yes, disappeared, vanished. It was unclear where he had gone, and people couldn't be sure whether he was alive or dead. Some had been startled by his sudden appearance from time to time in the years that followed, but most people thought those occasional sightings had been of his ghost—if you are patient, you'll get an explanation about that, too.

Without his grandfather around and having such a lout for a father as he did, with truly no other family to speak of, Mat Dawuk grew up like an orphaned kitten or a feral chicken, belonging to no one. He didn't go to school and no instructor in any of the prayer houses in the surrounding villages claimed to have ever taught him, though people often came across him roaming around the school grounds or crouching behind the mosque. Maybe he was trying to find a friend, but there weren't even any children willing to get close to him.

Of course, one or two kind-hearted people would offer him food or drink or buy the firewood that he would gather in the forest once he began to get bigger and was strong enough to haul it. But they wouldn't let their children get friendly with him. Mat Dawuk had never hurt another child or endangered anyone—at least, not at that point he hadn't—but still, parents used his filthy clothes, eerie silence and ugly face to frighten their kids.

'If you don't take your bath, you'll end up looking like Mat Dawuk. Is that what you want?' That's what they would say. Or, 'If you keep being so naughty, Mat Dawuk will come and snatch you up!' But the little children didn't need warnings like that to keep their distance. Even those his age were afraid. They didn't feel safe near him.

Then, his useless jerk of a father died too, flattened by an *Indonesia* bus en route from Semarang to Surabaya. Now, Mat Dawuk truly had nobody at all. The house his grandfather had left behind in Deep Well was neglected and had fallen into disrepair, but more neglected and beyond repair was Mat Dawuk's destiny. From a baby kitten without a mother, he grew into a wild dog without a master. It was no longer clear where he lived or whom he asked for food. Sometimes, he could be found on the front porch of an empty dwelling in Cottonwood Grove or Deep Well or huddling in quiet prayer house foyers that weren't already crowded with other sleeping kids, or playing alone in the schoolyard after classes were done for the day. But people also often found him roaming about in the forest or the Cottonwood Grove cemetery. If a kind-hearted person came upon him and asked what he was doing, Mat Dawuk's response was always the same. If he were in the forest, he would say, 'I'm looking for my grandfather.' If he were in the cemetery, he would say, 'I want to be near my mother.'

There must still have been those who took pity on him but most people, if asked, would have preferred that he just went away. And that's what happened—at some point, Mat Dawuk vanished. He could no longer be seen in the fields or gardens of Cottonwood Grove or wandering in the forest, in the graveyard, in the schoolyard or on prayer-house verandas. Nor was he in any of the surrounding villages.

Because his presence wasn't considered important, his disappearance wasn't made into an issue either. If he suddenly crossed their minds, people might say, 'He must have hopped one of those big trucks to Surabaya, or maybe Jakarta.'

Or someone might guess, 'Maybe he went into the jungle and was eaten by a leopard.' They would add, 'Poor guy…' but their tone sounded hopeful.

Because for such a long time there had been no news of him, those guesses that leaned towards wishes were then taken for the truth: Mat Dawuk must be dead. It was that way for years—until one, two and then three people who had come home from Malaysia said they had seen a young man whose face and demeanour reminded them of Mat Dawuk. He was showing up in different places. One had seen him in Kuala Lumpur. One had passed by him in Melaka. One had ridden in the same train car with him to Kedah. There was even someone who had accidentally happened upon him in Penang. As more people shared such stories, the supposition of his death, which up until this point had been agreed upon, started to dissolve.

And it turned out the stories were true—the guy they had seen in Malaysia really was Mat Dawuk. More precisely, the *man* they had seen, since Mat Dawuk was now well past adolescence. You'd better believe it—I even came across him there once myself.

As more and more people saw him, new stories began to replace the old. He would appear lurking in a certain shadowy corner of the train station, or waiting at a bus stop, never looking any better than how they remembered him. In adulthood, he let his hair grow long and curly and matted, never washed or combed, sometimes tied back, sometimes left loose to be blown by the wind. His face changed from ugly to menacing.

The most recognizable aspect of his appearance was his clothes: his black undershirt, the checkered button-down hanging from his bony shoulders and the ratty, stained, cream-coloured cargo pants with large pockets. Rumour had it those large pockets concealed a knife or short sword. Of course, people talk nonsense. Only later did they realize that what was really in the pocket of those Camel pants was a small pair of nunchucks—a weapon that consists of two sticks joined by a chain, rope or rawhide—or at least, something of that nature.

But whatever was in Mat Dawuk's pants pocket, people had grown even more afraid of him. Many felt certain that he had been involved in—or at the very least, could be connected to—the deaths of several Indonesians working overseas in Malaysia, and possibly two Indians and someone from Vietnam or Taiwan. He was a killer for hire; that was the rumour among the people from Cottonwood Grove living abroad in Malaysia, and even though you have to take anything a person from Cottonwood Grove says with a grain of salt, in this case, you'd better believe them. Yes, Mat Dawuk could be hired to kill. If it was a matter of revenge, an unpaid debt or a romantic dispute—for example, if you were a husband who wanted to teach your wife's boyfriend a lesson, or you wanted to hurt your girlfriend's husband, or you were a furious wife who wanted to give your wayward husband a good thrashing—then you could contact him and ask for his help. People even went as far as to discuss the price of Mat Dawuk's services—they were cheap, about one paycheck if you were hauling stones for construction, or one and a half if you worked as a housemaid. If Mat Dawuk thought the 'request for help' was justified but you came up short, he would be willing to take whatever you could pay, or he might even do it for free. And that was why people trembled when they saw him from a distance or even heard his name mentioned.

People who couldn't avoid him tried to stay on his good side and treated him well—something that he had hardly ever experienced before, not in his entire life. But for reasons unknown, Mat Dawuk still usually chose to keep to himself.

What people were sure of, what was no longer a question, was that Mat Dawuk, who had been such an ugly and forlorn kid, had become what we call a *dukdeng*, a powerful man, perhaps even invincible. But where could he have gotten his power? Had it been sent straight down from the heavens, or had he inherited it from his grandfather, the old guerrilla fighter Mbah Dulawi? And if so, how—since, by the time he was five years old, his grandfather had already vanished? Or, like most of the tough guys roaming around Malaysia, had he bought his supernatural powers and invincibility from one of the many sorcerers who can be found anywhere from Banten to Banyuwangi, if you know where to look? Or, as those who didn't believe any of that liked to scoff, was this just the image he cultivated to make himself seem intimidating? No one was sure. I myself don't know.

With all of this, though, nothing invited more speculation than the question: how did Mat Dawuk, who was withdrawn, hideous, frightening and rumoured to be a contract killer, meet Inayatun, who was beautiful, comely and fought over by so many men?

All sorts of ideas were proposed. Some were certain Mat Dawuk had forced himself on Inayatun, but most thought he had cast a spell on her, bewitched her with potions and charms—maybe Semar Mesem or Jaran Goyang, love magic from Banyuwangi or some other esoteric incantations that ordinary folks don't know much about. But what made the most sense was what Inayatun herself told people, and which luckily reached my ear.

She said that they were brought together by a murder. A murder that Mat Dawuk swore to Inayatun would be his last.

In Malaysia

'To bring that first meeting to light, let us return to Inayatun. But first, can I get a light? My cigarette's gone out.'

When Warto said that, I noticed my own cigarette had turned to ash too, I'd been so engrossed. My coffee cup was empty too, but I didn't have a chance to order another because he'd already resumed his story.

Inayatun hadn't even been in Malaysia for ten months, and she was already married—not legally, of course. She wasn't yet seventeen. The first man who took her for his wife was none other than the workforce manager who had dispatched her to Malaysia. He was very wealthy, that's what people knew about him. He owned multiple houses and multiple cars and—as you might have easily guessed—had multiple wives, too. Maybe because of this, he didn't have enough time or energy for Inayatun. But Inayatun was still in the bloom of youth and, filled with insatiable desire, it was a challenging situation for her to bear. Unsatisfied and feeling out of place, Inayatun made trouble. She got together with someone else. Her boss husband welcomed the new man, and Inayatun, without much thought, decided to leave and marry him instead.

But she had chosen her second husband practically at random and quickly grew bored with him. Moreover, the guy was still caring for a wife and kid back in his home village. His earnings as a construction labourer in Malaysia were enough to provide for them, but left little for Inayatun. It would have been hard enough if all she had needed was an allowance for lipstick and face powder, but Inayatun was beautiful, high-maintenance and the only job she had was running a tiny counter in a workplace cafeteria—it had grown quite popular once she started running it, still, to her the job was more like playing pretend than serious work. Given this underwhelming situation, a tantalizing offer from a contractor, a native Malaysian with Indian blood, quickly turned Inayatun's head.

He became her third husband, but he was a bit different from the other men Inayatun had been with. He had married her to save face in front of his buttoned-up business partners and Indonesian subordinates but he wasn't really interested in women, not even one as beautiful as Inayatun. He preferred the embrace of young men, what people here call *wandu*. Showered with wealth and finery, living in a palatial house but without love, Inayatun rebelled. She conspired with one of the contractor's lovers, one even younger than she was, and they ran away together.

Inayatun was free from her latest husband, and he didn't come looking for her, but she had fallen into the clutches of an immature youth who wanted to be obliged.

The kid said he preferred women but had sold himself to the contractor for the money. He wanted Inayatun to marry him. She was attracted to him, sure. The kid was handsome and full of passion—passion, mind you, what Inayatun hadn't gotten from her third husband. But, to get legally married? She felt it was better to wait. A woman as beautiful as Inayatun was used to being supported, whining and being indulged, making demands and being obeyed, not vice-versa. And she felt she had the right to act that way. She wasn't materialistic, no—she wasn't really interested in money; that hadn't been why she went all the way to Malaysia, and that wasn't why she coupled up so easily. She didn't want to be put out. So, whenever she eventually got legally married, she wanted it to be to an established man, one who could provide her with whatever she needed, whatever she wanted, whatever a woman of her beauty was entitled to. And that was why the immature guy who ran away with her was far from her ideal husband.

He was still a teenager, still volatile. He cursed everything in the world that had plunged him into misery as he had gone from being a village kid trying to prove he could contribute to his family's finances, to a hard-on-his-luck migrant who could only survive by selling his ass. The kid was down and out—he didn't have a job, work certificates or papers, which meant he couldn't even support himself. In his mind, the only thing that could redeem him was being with Inayatun. Meanwhile, it was obvious to Inayatun that she couldn't rely on the kid nor expect much of him—he was only good as a lover. He could not be more.

Inayatun tried to leave, but she had truly taken up with the wrong man this time. The kid loved Inayatun to death, wanted to marry her, wanted to control her, would do anything to make Inayatun stay—or, more precisely, he would do anything to ensure Inayatun couldn't go anywhere. Inayatun now had a big problem. Her first attempt at leaving ended in violence. He beat her, called her a cheap whore with no sense of gratitude who didn't know what love was. The more Inayatun fought back, the more he harmed her. The harder she sought help, the worse she was treated.

And so, while Inayatun initially thought they had both escaped, she ended up captured and trapped. (This was the worst thing that had ever happened to her so far, although much worse would befall her after she returned home.)

Finally, Inayatun was desperate. Battered and bruised, fighting for her life, she escaped. Imagine a scene in a Bollywood film where the heroine is being chased by bad guys—that's more or less the state she was in. And it is exactly at this point that our hero—or an even more terrifying villain, it all depends on what you want to call him—appears.

The Meeting

I DIDN'T WITNESS their meeting with my own eyes, so I don't know exactly how it happened. But someone I trust knows all about it and told me the story. And now, I'm going to tell it to you. It happened like this…

Inayatun had just collapsed onto a chair in a secluded corner of a waiting room in a small deserted train station near Kuala Lumpur—I don't think the name of the exact spot is important, and anyway, I don't remember. She was trembling with fear, her face was all bruised and she'd been wearing the same dress for days. Her hands clutched a small bag in her lap. At that moment, someone called her name.

'Ina!'

It was Mat Dawuk—maybe the first time he had spoken before being spoken to, and indeed the first time he had ever spontaneously greeted a woman.

Approached by a man who cut such an unpleasant figure, Inayatun shuddered and shrunk away as anyone would.

'It's Inayatun, right?' Mat Dawuk asked. 'Mat. I'm

Mat.' He gathered his long, curly hair back to give her a better look at his ugly face. 'Cottonwood Grove. I'm from Cottonwood Grove.'

Inayatun knew the name of the village, of course, then remembered his name, and after a long while, began to recognize the face before her. It wasn't pleasant to look at—who could stand Mat Dawuk's face? But, at the same time, Inayatun found refuge in his eyes, the feeling of safety she had been searching for. It wasn't the expression she was used to seeing when men looked at her, and it immediately soothed her. She burst into tears.

Mat Dawuk was at a loss. What were you supposed to do with a sobbing woman? Embrace her, stroke her shoulder, hold her hand or maybe say words of comfort? He should do something—but how could Mat Dawuk do anything like that? He wasn't just unaccustomed to crying women; he wasn't accustomed to women at all. He wasn't accustomed to anybody.

Even so, he could guess what had happened to her. This wasn't the first time he had encountered a Javanese woman crying on a bench in a Malaysian train station; it could mean all kinds of things, but just about all of them were bad. Maybe her husband had been arrested by Malaysian police because his papers weren't in order. Maybe her family member had died in an accident at work, and nobody cared. Maybe she had been tricked by some bastard—her lover, her common-law husband or a man she had just met. Maybe she was being chased by someone sent by her lover's wife or her husband's girlfriend. And there were plenty of other unpleasant possibilities, so he simply sat down one seat away from Inayatun, tried to show her with little gestures that he was no threat, and waited for her sobs to subside—and for whatever was about to happen next.

Sure enough, about half an hour later, a man appeared, his eyes darting this way and that as he scanned the station.

When Inayatun saw him and Mat Dawuk saw the terror in her eyes, he understood everything. Without words, he gave Inayatun a sign that she didn't have to be afraid or run.

'Who you looking for, brother?' Mat Dawuk called out in an east Javanese dialect, in a tone that was asking for trouble. The man looked over for a moment and then hurried towards Inayatun with arms outstretched. Like a man who has just spotted his misplaced treasure, like a lion who has cornered the deer he has been stalking, he advanced, ready to pounce—but his movements were halted as from behind a pair of hands grabbed his shoulders at the base of his neck.

'Who you looking for, brother?' Mat Dawuk asked again. He used the same tone of voice, but as he spoke, he was tightening the grip of his left hand around the man's neck, his thumb planted right in the man's shoulder joint, preventing him from moving forward but also from turning around.

'She's my wife, so stay out of it!' the man sputtered angrily, struggling to get loose.

'She's my sister, so don't be so rough,' Mat Dawuk replied, still digging his left thumb into the guy's right shoulder. Of course, Mat Dawuk wasn't trying to calm the man down or make him listen to reason—he wanted to rile him up.

The plan worked. The man struggled with all his might, trying to free his right shoulder and jab his left fist. But an angry man was a tasty treat for Mat Dawuk, who deftly caught the furious left hand throwing a punch with his right hand, twisting it as easily as wringing out a piece of wet laundry. For the first time, the predator and the saviour faced each other, for a brief moment, and it is easy to guess who trembled to see who. But the standoff didn't last long because one of the men—of course, I don't mean Mat Dawuk—was lifted into the air, swung around, spun and slammed onto the station floor. Imagine a closed fan that is unfurled in a flash and closed again. That's more or less what it looked like, just on a slightly bigger scale.

There was a loud 'crack' as the man's leg slammed into the edge of the bench Inayatun was crouching on. She screamed and recoiled. A group of Malaysian women waiting for their train screamed, too, but they shut their mouths and quickly scattered when Mat Dawuk gestured for them to stay out of it—in any case, if two Indonesians were fighting over a woman, it was better to leave and pray they both died in the altercation.

Mat Dawuk turned to Inayatun, to signal to her to calm down rather than scream and invite attention, and to reassure her that the situation was under control, but Inayatun shouted, 'Mat! Look out!'

The guy was trying to get up and fight back. Still doubled over in pain, he hurled his body at Mat Dawuk's legs with a knife he had pulled from somewhere. Inayatun's warning came just in time. Even though he was caught off guard, Mat Dawuk was able to jump back, and the attacker stabbed only empty air. Before the attacker could right himself, Mat Dawuk swung his right foot squarely into the guy's jaw. It looked just like the volleykick of a striker scoring a beautiful distance goal—have you seen the goal Van Basten put into the net of the Soviet Union in the '88 Euro Cup Final? It was just like that. And like a kicked ball, the attacker's body flew two metres back before he fell head first onto the station floor. His knife went flying, too. A few of his teeth had been knocked out, and blood trickled out from the corner of his mouth.

Mat Dawuk leaned his ugly face down close to the man, now helplessly sprawled out and gasping for breath. 'If you dare come looking for Inayatun again,' he threatened, 'you'll wind up dead!'

Then Mat Dawuk looked towards Inayatun and with a cock of his chin, said, 'Come on, I'll take you home.' But she just sat there, petrified. Mat Dawuk repeated the invitation, but Inayatun remained frozen where she sat. She didn't have any place to go. She could have asked Mat Dawuk to take her to some distant relations who lived in Damansara or to a friend's place in Petaling Jaya, but of course, it wasn't easy to decide in such a state. She wasn't sure her family or her friend would even take her in, but worse, she was worried that the man who was now collapsed at her feet would come looking for her, find her and hurt her.

'Where do you live?'

Inayatun was unresponsive.

'I see. Just come with me.' But his tone was gentle.

After remaining still as a stone for one more moment, Inayatun hesitantly rose, putting one foot in front of another to follow Mat Dawuk. A while later, a train arrived, and the pair was swallowed up by its closing doors.

So, that's how they met, and that meeting would lead to big changes in their lives...and, of course, to their deaths.

A Peculiar Couple

A LIGHTER, WHO has a lighter?

I wouldn't mind another cigarette. Aha...

After that meeting, Inayatun stayed at Mat Dawuk's place, in an unfinished two-storey building on the edge of a palm plantation belonging to FELDA (The Federal Land Development Authority, that's what Malay people call it, it's the organization that takes care of agriculture in Malaysia, or at least, as far as I know). The place was occupied by Mat Dawuk and three other men—an Indian he called Ambu and two workers from Myanmar whose names were hard to pronounce, so he just called them Upstairs Burma and Downstairs Burma, according to their rooms. When Inayatun asked him why he didn't stay with migrants from Cottonwood Grove or at least with other Javanese, biting his lip—his hideous lip—Mat Dawuk replied that he got along better with these foreigners than most of the folks from Cottonwood Grove or Java. 'They don't ask so many questions,' he said.

Of course, they didn't. The two from Myanmar could barely speak Malay, even though they had worked in

Malaysia for years. 'But they pray diligently—yeah, they're Muslim.' That was the extent of Mat Dawuk's elaboration. Meanwhile, Ambu, the Indian, had learned a bit of Malay but only talked to Mat Dawuk about music. 'He can sing like a woman, like Lata Mangeshkar; his voice is so sweet,' Mat Dawuk said. 'And he can turn anything into a drum.'

Mat Dawuk's quarters were far neater than you would have imagined from his appearance. Of course, the room was fairly modest, just a square patch of drywall and asbestos, three metres by two metres, in an unfinished building at the edge of a derelict field. The floor was rough plaster, hastily spread to cover the shoddily poured concrete. There wasn't anything of much interest inside, as was fitting for the room of a migrant worker, who had to be ready to pack up and leave at a moment's notice should difficult circumstances arise.

The first time Inayatun entered the room, there was nothing there but a small day bed with a thin mattress propped up on three layers of particleboard and a pillow and bolster stacked beside a low table—neatly painted and draped with a small tablecloth, people could never notice that it was built by hand out of scrap wood. On the table was a small tape player with its deck open, a cassette inside—clearly frequently used. Not far from the cassette player, so that it could be reached by whoever might be lying on the bed, a tiny shelf was nailed into the wall, holding a neat row of cassettes, all soundtracks from Bollywood films. On the wall above the head of the bed hung a poster; whoever entered the room would find themselves staring at a blood-spattered Sunny Deol, with his small eyes and large hands, his muscles bulging out of a black singlet, his weapon hung at his hip à la Rambo, rage emanating from his face, the bold lettering of the film title *Ghayal* beneath him.

Another poster, displaying a much calmer scene, was hung on the opposite wall so that whoever lay on the day bed could gaze at it for as long as they pleased. Sunny Deol again, but this time with melancholy eyes and the clothes of a Gujarat cow herder (who knows from what era). Poonam Dhillon, her face framed by the graceful folds of her veil, leaned back against his broad chest. *Sohni Mahiwal* was written across the bottom in a greenish yellow. That was the title of the film. (Have you ever seen it? Ah, the story is so sad.) Across from the day bed, stuck to the other wall, was another shelf, holding books. There weren't very many—what hard labourer collects books? In addition to a Quran, which looked old and unopened, there were a few dusty volumes with Arabic titles and a pile of *Wiro Sableng* martial arts serials. Above this was another poster—not another movie poster, but Arabic calligraphy. Behind the door was a row of hooks where Mat Dawuk's clothes hung. Underneath sat a backpack and a heap of travel gear. That was where some more of Mat Dawuk's clothes and everything else he owned in this world was stored. Don't ask if there was a cupboard in that room; there wasn't one. What would it be for? Impractical.

'You sleep here,' Mat Dawuk said, pointing to the day bed. 'I don't have anywhere else. Sorry, it's such a mess.'

'And you…?'

'I'll be fine.'

'But...'

'Don't worry. That kid won't dare show up here.'

Ina sat down on the day bed, weak and spent but still looking curiously around the room. 'May I...' She pointed to the cassette player on the table.

'If you'd like, sure,' Mat Dawuk smiled—though, trust me, a smile did nothing for his looks.

Inayatun rummaged through Mat's tapes.

'Do you have the *Betaab* soundtrack?' The terror she had felt when they first met had gone. She felt quite at home.

Mat Dawuk smiled wider. 'Two copies. One is pirated from Kuching Records. The other one is original and was imported straight from India. Ambu gave it to me. But a kid from Lerok village back home borrowed the Kuching one, and he hasn't returned it. Maybe it's lost. And the other one I lent to Upstairs Burma. If you want, I can ask for it.'

Then Mat Dawuk took his leave, promising he would quickly return with medicine for the cuts and bruises on Inayatun's face and a few items of clothing she could wear for the time being.

Of course, it was far more basic than what she was used to back home or in Malaysia, but Inayatun liked Mat's room. If all the other houses she had lived in made her feel catered to, this place made her feel protected. Nothing would bother her here. No one would harass her. She didn't know whether Mat Dawuk knew about her or her preferences, but she felt like the room had been made for her. Its Bollywood film posters made her feel welcome and accepted, just as she was. And after she had stayed there for almost a week, Inyatun felt herself start to regain control—of her thoughts and body.

But then, one night, a thudding commotion startled her awake from a fitful sleep. It was right outside. Fearfully, she peeked out of the window from behind a piece of fabric haphazardly tacked up over a trellis made from three crooked planks. She couldn't tell what was happening out there, what she was seeing. Her eyes could only catch glimpses of movement—rolling here and there, jumping, darting from one place to another, from the branch of one palm tree to another, from the ground to the treetops and back down again—and she could only catch incoherent yells and groans, and a whirring sound that rose and fell. Then, another scream and a moan. And then silence.

Before she could determine what it was, the commotion that had awoken her subsided—or almost subsided. She heard another moan, softer now. Her eyes were still heavy with sleep and reluctant with fear, but she forced herself to get a better look. Squinting into the patches of moonlight and the weak illumination from the lamp hanging in front of the house, she could see four men sprawled on the ground, one of them wracked with convulsions. Beyond them, she could barely make out a figure standing over them. He was breathing heavily but didn't look at all spent. With both feet planted firmly on the ground, he rose tall and strong above the four collapsed bodies, his right hand by his side, a strange weapon in its grip (later, she learned it was a nunchuck), his left hand still clenched into a mighty fist. The moonlight reflected off his long, curly hair, but his face, shrouded by the shadows of the palm leaves, seemed a gaping black hole. If the angel of death had assumed a human form, maybe it wouldn't look too different. He—the man still standing—was Mat Dawuk.

The convulsing man was now wholly motionless, curled up in the foetal position. 'Take him away!' Mat ordered, bending over to shake the other men lying there groaning. 'Bury him properly!'

From her secret vantage point, Ina could see the stilled figure, and the nape of his neck was wet with a blackish liquid that gleamed in the moonlight. It was too dim for her to see his face, but she was not unfamiliar with the shape of his body or his clothes. It was the youth who had run away with her, demanded she marry him and then attacked her. The kid must have somehow tracked her down and, bringing the three other men as backup, had come for her. And he had faced the consequences.

'Hey!' Mat Dawuk snapped when he saw the three men scrambling to their feet and making to run away. 'Take your friend with you!' Lifting his right hand and twirling his weapon, he growled, 'Or I'll bury you all with him!'

The men, visibly injured, hurriedly and with great difficulty dragged away the corpse. In her room, Ina collapsed weakly down onto the day bed, trembling, just as she had sat in fear in the Kuala Lumpur train station two weeks ago. She had seen for herself: the man who had attacked her was dead. He could no longer threaten her, but now she realized the kind of man she was currently living with. The last guy had been rough, forced her into things and was quick to hit. But this man who had helped her, in whose eyes Ina had found protection and a feeling of sanctuary, could kill with ease.

It was as if the black on the corpse's neck had glistened so brightly it had forced her eyes shut, as if Mat Dawuk's growled threat had left her ears ringing. The safety and protection she had enjoyed for the past two weeks was gone. As she sat there, shuddering, her thoughts consumed with blood glimmering in the moonlight, Mat Dawuk's kindness and gentleness, his shy and respectful character, disappeared, and the stories she had heard long ago in her childhood about the man who had helped her—which until now she had forgotten—all came rushing back. Her mother's threat when she had been a stubborn child who refused to take a bath and was lazy about saying her prayers: 'If you don't wash, Mat Dawuk will snatch you up and carry you to the graveyard!' Or her father's rebuke when she had grown into an impertinent young girl who came home late from prayer recitation: 'Only when Mat Dawuk has you by the neck will you come to your senses!' She had ignored those warnings, just as she had ignored all the warnings about the kid, but now she could see why the children of Cottonwood Grove feared Mat Dawuk.

She should run from this place, escape this savage killer—she hurried to the door, opened it and collided with Mat Dawuk, who was on his way inside.

'It's over. You don't have to be afraid anymore.' To reassure her, Mat Dawuk put his hand on Inayatun's shoulder—the first time he had ever touched her. But Inayatun recoiled, horrified to see his fingers smeared with blood.

She gulped. 'Are you…' she seemed to crumple, her lips quivering and her body shaking, 'Are you…going to kill me too?'

Now Mat Dawuk knew who Inayatun was afraid of. So, he stepped back too, giving her space, discreetly wiping the blood off his right hand with his shirt sleeve and then letting both hands fall to his sides and hang there, like a surrendered convict awaiting his sentence. Then, after clearing his throat twice, he answered softly and tentatively: 'I…I only kill people for a good reason.'

'So…' Still, trembling, Inayatun asked, 'If you had a good reason, you would kill me?'

Mat Dawuk shook his head weakly. 'No.' Then, head still shaking, he slumped down to the floor, his gaze sinking to his knees. He stayed silent for a long time.

So did Inayatun.

'No,' Mat Dawuk said again finally, this time with a more emphatic shake of his head. 'Even if I had one thousand reasons, I would never kill you.' Then he stood up as if to leave.

'Where are you going?' Inayatun asked. The tone of her voice had changed a little.

'I have to clean up all evidence of the fight. I want everything in order before my roommates get home,' Mat Dawuk replied, backing away.

'Where are they?'

'Working overtime.'

'When you're done, will you come right back?'

He paused. 'Maybe I'll go out for a while. Or maybe I won't come back until tomorrow.'

'Why?'

Quiet again. Then, 'I'm going to find you another place to live, somewhere better.'

'Why?'

'Well, don't I...don't I scare you?'

Inayatun realized her mistake and softly shook her head. 'Clean up the blood. After that, please come back. I'm scared to be alone.'

Inayatun returned to the day bed and waited for Mat Dawuk's return.

Overwhelmed and exhausted, she lay down and soon fell back asleep. A nightmare startled her awake, and she found Mat Dawuk sitting on the edge of the day bed, holding out a glass of water.

'Drink,' he said. 'You don't have to be afraid.'

Inayatun took the water and drank.

'Where did you go? You took so long.'

'I came back, and you had already fallen asleep, so I stood guard outside the door. Now, get some more rest. I'll watch over you.' Mat Dawuk got up to leave.

'What about you?'

'I'll be guarding the door.'

Mat Dawuk went out and was about to close the door when Inayatun beckoned him back.

'You can sleep inside,' she blurted out, 'if it's not too much trouble.'

Mat Dawuk left and, a few moments later, came back with a bamboo mat. He rolled it out on the floor and lay down. When he awoke early, he found Inayatun nestled against his back.

They soon got used to that, and after a while, maybe out of a growing need, what was inevitably going to happen, happened—you know what I mean, right?

Because he felt guilty about what they had done, Mat Dawuk took down the Arabic calligraphy, rolled it up and put it into a cardboard box, along with his old Quran and Arabic books. He only put the poster back up after they had been living together for four months, and after much persuasion, he had accepted Inayatun's marriage proposal.

They were married by one of Mat's co-workers, who had been his teacher at a madrasa in Lerok, a village not far from Cottonwood Grove. In terms of outward appearances, they were a peculiar couple. But their union felt perfectly natural to them—they felt like they had been made for each other. They believed they had been fated to meet—to complete, fulfil, heal one another.

Mat calmed Inayatun down, making her feel in control and self-controlled, that's what she said. While Inayatun led Mat out of the loneliness and misery he had been living in his entire life, more or less that's how he felt. Like a basket that had found its lid, a dipper that had found a barrel of cool water, and of course, like a mortar that had found its pestle, they fit together.

After they had lived together for seven months, Mat once again removed his calligraphy poster from the wall. He also removed his Quran and other books from the shelf, put them into a cardboard box, and wrapped them up neatly. This time, his film posters, *Wiro Sableng* books, and Indian music cassettes were in the box, too: the couple had decided to go home to Cottonwood Grove.

'It's for a better life,' that's how they put it when they said their goodbyes to their friends and acquaintances in Malaysia.

But, as you all know, it was their destruction that was lying in wait.

The Cozy Shed

THIS IS THE happiest part of the dark tale I am telling you. So, come on, let's begin this part with a song:

Jab hum jawaan honge, jaane kahaan honge
Jab hum jawaan honge, jaane kahaan honge
Lekin jahaan honge, waha fariyaad karenge
Tujhe yaad karenge…

What, none of you know this song at all? Really?

My God, so what is it that you all listen to? Let me guess…it must be that awful *dangdut* stuff, right? Yeah, okay, what can I do, let's move on.

The short version is: that's the song that was often heard coming from their cozy cow shed, where they made their home after returning to Cottonwood Grove. That's the song Lata Mangeshkar and Shabbir Kumar sing in the film *Betaab*, starring Amrita Singh and Sunny Deol.

Ugh, don't tell me you haven't heard of this film either. I can't take it. All along the northern coast of Java, from Serang to Pasuruan, people were crazy over it; if I'm not mistaken, it was in 1984. Cinema Mandala Yuda, which doesn't show films anymore, played it for three months straight, and the songs were on all the radio stations, night and day. *Jab Hum Jawaan Honge* was the most famous, the other ones were good too.

I called their house a cozy 'cow shed' because that is the correct term for the place they moved into when they arrived in Cottonwood Grove. It was literally an old cow shed belonging to Pak Imam, who was forced to give it to his headstrong daughter and her ugly new husband. It was a bit remote, even from the outskirts of the town, close to the forest, and it was abandoned and hadn't been used for years. Pak Imam was furious at his daughter's arrival and at losing face in the village thanks to her hideous new husband. He would have given Inayatun however much it took for them to return to Malaysia—or go anywhere at all, as long as they didn't stay and embarrass the family. But Inayatun was not shaken by a storm, not damped by rain, not parched by searing heat. She was obstinate, just as always. She wasn't going anywhere—*they* weren't going anywhere—except Cottonwood Grove, that's what she vowed. She would live in her homeland, in the town where she was born, with Mat Dawuk, with or without her father's blessing.

'If you won't offer us a room in your house or gift us a plot of land, we can roll out our mat in front of the mosque or pitch a tent on the veranda of the town hall,' Inayatun had said in complete earnest.

Afraid his child would follow through on her threats as she had done before, Pak Imam was forced to give them the old cow shed in the middle of the forest. His hope was that they wouldn't like it there, and after a while would flee, get out and go far, far away.

But, as always, when Pak Imam tried to guess what was in his daughter's head, he was wrong. Not a total trash heap, that old cow shed seemed like a love palace to Ina and Mat, and even more so after Mat restored it; he replaced the torn and peeling old walls with newly plaited bamboo, neatly re-set the roof tiles, added a thatched roof over the kitchen and veranda, fenced the yard with bamboo and planted it with beans and vegetables for them to eat, got a few chickens to wander around and with the little money left over from what they had brought from Malaysia, bought a pet goat.

'This is just like the shed in *Betaab*. Spacious and quiet,' Inayatun said, her eyes shining, one afternoon after they made love on the floor because they hadn't finished putting the bed-frame together. 'We're the Sunny and Roma of Cottonwood Grove.'

Any way you looked at it, they didn't fit together. They were irreconcilable opposites and they should never have met, like the earth and the sky, like the shining point of the farthest star and the muddy pit of the deepest well, like rain and laundry hung out to dry.

'But we don't have a stable full of horses like they did in *Betaab*. Just one goat,' Mat replied.

'What do I need with a horse? I already have you,' Inayatun said, straddling Mat's belly with her usual mischievous smile and roving hands.

'You are just as beautiful as Roma.' Mat's rough hands caressed Inayatun's smooth face. 'But I'm a far cry from Sunny.'

'Don't you know that you look like Sunny?'

'Is that so?'

'Yeah, after he's been beaten by his enemies when he's wounded and all in a state!'

Mat's squinty eyes widened in mock anger. 'Making fun of me, are you? You'd better watch out; I bite when provoked!'

Inayatun jumped up and ran away with little shrieks. Mat went after her. They chased each other all around their cozy shed. Mat caught up with her and threw his arms around her. Inayatun laughed, but she quickly shook him off and escaped again. And Mat chased her again. And as soon as she was caught again, they were locked in an embrace. They were truly happy, and their happiness radiated throughout the entire clearing on the edge of the forest. After witnessing those two together, the finches nestled, male lizards pursued the females in the bushes, a rooster stamped his feet and crowed for the hen who might become the mother of his next brood of chicks, and behind the house, a pair of squirrels mated high in the branches of a moringa tree. The goat, who didn't have a partner, rubbed its rump against the stable wall.

And make no mistake, that happiness spread even further. The isolation of the place couldn't contain it. The dense bushes, the narrow footpath and the clusters of banana trees fell under its sway. There were about four garden plots and two empty yards between that cozy shed and the nearest neighbour, and the path heading into the forest was about as far away. But, even at that distance, the neighbours and the passersby heading for the forest would certainly have heard the music coming from the old cow shed turned love shack. And they would undoubtedly have heard Inayatun's giggles as, tickled by Mat Dawuk, she imitated the laughter of Lata Mangeshkar in the song I sang for you earlier.

What's more, it had long been Inayatun's nature, ever since she was an infamous underaged girl known by the nickname Ina Indomilk, the virgin milk peddler, to flaunt the fact that she was happier than most other women in Cottonwood Grove. Perhaps she did it unconsciously. She had rarely socialized since coming home from Malaysia, in part because her house was far from town but mostly because she felt her initial appearance at the mosque with Mat Dawuk to join in congregational prayer had been too conspicuous, and she was reluctant to once again become the centre of attention.

Even so, at least every other day, she went to the village market to buy fish or salt or barter the vegetables from her yard or the flame-of-the-forest petals that she had foraged for sugar, coffee or salt. And whenever she appeared on the village road or was spotted at the market gate, she still triggered the same agitation as when she was a teenager—or worse.

Before, with the airs she put on, whenever she passed by, all the bachelors in the *warung* would put down their cups of coffee and flick on their cigarette lighters, and all the mothers would worry about the faith and morals of their full-grown sons. It wasn't that different now—in fact, it was even more obvious that when she came around, husbands grew dissatisfied with their wives, and their wives grew unhappy. She wasn't as made up as before, wearing almost no face powder and usually no lipstick, but that didn't diminish her glamour. If her arms held bundles of long beans or she had a roll of banana or teak leaves on her hip, this only seemed to bestow an even more intoxicating charm upon her. Like aged palm wine, that's what the men in the *warung* would say. Some would go even further to compare her to a forest nymph out of a fairy tale—bedecked in green, lost in the village, caught in the daylight and unable to go home.

On top of that, she always appeared with her face shining and hair wet, which could only mean one thing. Now, come on, what wife wouldn't be uneasy?

'Don't you get cold, Ina, washing your hair every morning?' a yam seller asked, but it sounded like an insult.

'Yes, it's cold, Yu. But what else can I do, not wash my hair? If I don't, the chickens will scold me, that's what the *kyai* say,' Inayatun replied.

'You can't possibly…every night,' the questioner mumbled before trailing off.

'Sometimes in the middle of the day, too, Yu,' Inayatun said.

The yam seller frowned. But Inayatun didn't stop. 'Might as well, while I'm still young!'

The frown on the face before her deepened.

Inayatun didn't care at all. 'Relax, Yu. I'm doing it with my husband!'

The yam seller shook her head. Inayatun just grinned, busy selecting the yams she would buy.

'Ina…'

'Yes, Yu?'

'What actually…' the woman hesitated but emboldened

herself, 'What actually do you see in Mat Dawuk?' Finally, out came the question that was on everyone's mind.

Inayatun gave a tight-lipped smile. She had known that sooner or later, she would have to answer that question. She picked up a thick, long tuber, and held it out to the yam seller.

'Does this taste good or not, Yu?' she asked.

'It does. All my yams are tasty, Ina. They're especially delicious boiled,' the seller answered.

'Really?' Inayatun smirked. 'It tastes good, even though it's so ugly?'

'It looks ugly, but when it's ripe and ready, well… it's soft and smooth, it practically melts in your mouth, especially if you eat it up while it's still hot,' the woman assured, hoping to make a sale.

'So then, it's just like my husband,' Inayatun replied softly but loud enough to be heard. 'Imagine, Yu,' Inayatun held the yam playfully, 'if this wasn't a yam. And it was warm and firm and toothsome, even though it hadn't been boiled.' Inayatun's smile changed from impertinent to wicked.

'Hey, what are we talking about here?' pouted the seller.

Inayatun, who was having a relapse of insolence, reached into a nearby bundle, snapped off a small and withered long bean, and held it out to the yam seller.

'If what you usually eat is nothing but a long bean, one that's already all shrivelled up at that, and you boil it until it's overcooked, well then it will be hard to understand how delicious a raw yam is, Yu.' Then Inayatun's smile vanished as she burst into laughter.

And the target of her laughter flushed a deep scarlet.

'So, how much do your delicious yams cost, Yu?'

'They're not for sale!'

'Do you want to try the one I have?'

'Pssshht! I wouldn't like it at all!'

Inayatun sauntered away, chuckling, leaving the yam seller to grumble and curse. And these sorts of incidents didn't just happen once or twice.

'It's not like there weren't enough handsome guys interested, so why'd you choose one like that, huh, Mbak In?' Another snide comment about Mat Dawuk. Usually, someone willing to be so blunt was younger.

'All the handsome ones were taken, little sis,' was Inayatun's classic answer.

'I guess so, but even someone as ugly as me got a handsome husband.' So it continued.

'Handsome leftovers, sure, little sis,' Inayatun would counter breezily.

'What do you mean leftovers?'

'Ask your husband.' Then Inayatun would smile and wink, and suddenly, the questioner would know precisely what she meant.

Sometimes, if the one being insulted refused to take it, there would be an argument. But, any woman who fought with Inayatun had to be quite clever; Inayatun could cut down the women of Cottonwood Grove as easily as she had confounded the men. And her method, of course, was always the same: mentioning their husbands.

Inayatun always claimed that a quarter of the men in Cottonwood Grove had tried to seduce her, and she had obliged at least half of those, and she knew what they liked better than their wives. After marrying Mat Dawuk, she vowed to stop being so easy. But sometimes, she still let her past slip out in conversation, or even, let's say, bragged about it.

Once that happened, the women would fall silent. Humph! Then, they would hurry home to berate their husbands.

When she was still a virgin, Inayatun had been looked at with suspicion. When she married Mat Dawuk, she became the subject of gossip. But really, she was not just a threat but a revelation for her people. Her every movement became the centre of attention, investigation, and discussion—and, of course, imitation. From Inayatun, the women of Cottonwood Grove learned what men wanted and what their husbands yearned for. Comparing themselves to Inayatun and feeling that they fell short, the women grew more diligent in their self-care. And from Inayatun, whether they admitted it or not, they ultimately learned how to be happier women and how to take pride in themselves. And Inayatun knew this all too well.

There was one bit of happiness, though, that she didn't want to share: a happiness that was only to be savoured in their fixed-up stable and nowhere else. Not even a bird might hear lest it spread the news to the entire forest. The wind must not carry it across the fields to Cottonwood Grove. Just she and Mat Dawuk alone should know. So, after they had made love, she murmured this happiness into his ear.

'I'm late.'

Mat didn't understand immediately.

'Earlier this morning, I threw up,' she whispered.

'So?' Mat was still confused.

'I'm pregnant, you dummy!' This time louder. 'You knocked me up!' she repeated, using her hand to trace the outline of a large belly.

Mat was shocked. Overjoyed but also concerned. 'Why didn't you say so before?'

'What do you mean before?'

'We shouldn't have…'

'What do you mean "shouldn't have"?'

'Is it permitted?'

'Up until now, have we done only what is permitted?'

'What I mean is, isn't it dangerous for the baby?'

'Is it forbidden in those *Wiro Sableng* books of yours?'

'How should I know? I can't read. You know I never went to school. Plus, those books weren't mine; they belonged to my Uncle.'

'You…can't read?'

'All I can read is what it says on my work permit. And my name, Muhammad Dawud. And your name, Inayatun Nikmah.' Mat Dawuk grinned.

'But what will become of my child if its father is illiterate?' she asked, smacking her forehead and stroking her belly, affecting a tragic air.

'It will be smart, of course!' Mat Dawuk declared.

'And how can that be?'

'Well, its mother was the star of the class.'

'How do you know?'

'Find me one person in all of Cottonwood Grove who hasn't heard of Inayatun.'

'What else do you know about me, huh?'

'Ask away!'

'What is my favourite Bollywood film?'

'That's easy, *Betaab*.'

'Because I listen to the soundtrack every day?'

'Because you used to watch it over and over. Over and over.'

'How do you know? Where did I watch it?'

'Umi Muslihati's house. You watched it with Haji Marsaid's second wife, on video.'

Inayatun's beautiful eyes narrowed. 'You used to spy on me, didn't you?' Mat Dawuk chuckled.

'Don't tell me you've had a crush on me ever since I was little?' Mat gave a hideous, coy smile.

'Oh...' Inayatun pretended to be furious. 'So it must be true what they say—you bewitched me, didn't you!?'

'Of course! Would you like me to break the spell?'

Inayatun smiled, shaking her head emphatically. 'Not at all!'

'So?'

'Entrance me again.'

'You haven't had enough?'

'Not yet.'

'And how should I do it?'

'Is there any other way?'

Mat was pensive for a moment. 'What about the baby?'

Inayatun answered with ravenous kisses. They grappled again, growing even happier. It was as if they were trying to take all the joy they could get, as if it would forever replenish—they wanted more and more and more.

Perhaps, somehow, they sensed it would not last much longer.

Happiness is Like a Cup of Coffee

Do you all know what happiness is?

Here. Look at this cup of coffee. Yup, this is happiness. Sooner or later, it will be finished—and the more delicious it is, the faster it will go. Sure, sometimes we really want to take our time and enjoy it, sipping it up little by little, holding it on our tongue, playing with it a little bit along the roof of our mouth, savouring it, not wanting to swallow it too quickly. But then, whoops! What do you know, as soon as we peer into the bottom of the cup, all that's left is the dregs. It's gone, and maybe because we in fact greedily gulped it down without realizing. Or maybe our careless hand or foot knocks the cup over and sends it rolling, and the coffee spills; what a waste. Or maybe some oaf comes and drinks it down without a care, leaving not even a drop behind for us.

What? What about the cup of coffee that never gets drunk, you ask? Well, coffee that doesn't get drunk is not coffee. It's just plain old water with a cursed fate.

This world is impermanent, my brothers and sisters. And it's not me who said that, it's God—please, you can look the verse up yourself. Everything will perish.

Everything! Water returns to water—dust to dust. Ultimately, there will be nothing left but empty air because, indeed, it is from the ether that the cosmos arose and life began. Happiness, as you all know, if it exists, is just a worldly deception, nothing more than a game. That's why God only promises happiness in the afterlife, not here, not in this world. That which is eternal, *khaalidiina fiha abadan*, is only in heaven. Here, everything is impermanent. And everything impermanent will perish. Die. Disappear.

Happiness is a marble, did you all know that? But even that round, clear and lustrous object that we fight for, that we fight over, that we weep over because we want it so badly, that we journey for and sweat over, in the end, will leave us with nothing but a scar. Happiness is nothing more than a kite that soars peacefully until its thread suddenly snaps—then it droops, falls and disappears to who knows where. Yes, everything will end sooner or later—or maybe far too soon. And many a happiness comes to a terrible end.

Just like the story I'm telling you right now.

But, by the way, in making this analogy, I've pointed to my cup of coffee and, as you can tell, all there is left is the grounds. Not one of you is moved to order me another? Even though it's impermanent and temporary, you think I don't want my share of happiness, huh?

Aha…yes, that's it, great. Siti! Another coffee, the usual!

All right then, let's get back to Mat and Inayatun's happiness.

After he learned about his wife's pregnancy, Mat Dawuk grew cautious. His love was ever strong, but now he was also unrelentingly overprotective. He forbade Inayatun to go to the market, at least for the time being; there was still enough rice, the chickens were laying eggs, fish could be caught in the shallow rivers in the forest, there was enough salt, there were still plenty of vegetables and her cravings for meat were best controlled for now anyway. If there were anything that was truly needed, Mat would insist on being the one to go get it. All Inayatun should do was get plenty of rest, eat good food, drink traditional health tonics, think good thoughts—and, most importantly, abstain as much as possible. That was what Mat Dawuk repeatedly advised.

The other thing Mat recommended his wife do was go to see her parents, tell them the news of her pregnancy, and ask for their prayers and blessings. Who knows whether such a thing might make her family—who had remained unrelenting regarding their marriage—yield a little. If they wouldn't accept him as their son-in-law, that was fine; the important thing was that they be on good terms with their daughter and, most importantly, accept their future grandchild-to-be. With an air of wisdom, he advised his wife that her discord with her parents should not be passed down to their future child. And if their relationship could be improved sooner, all the better, why put it off? Mat reminded Inayatun that, as this would be her first child, she would certainly need her mother when she went into labour.

But Inayatun, as always, casually shrugged and said that her parents would discover the news on their own, and with regard to labour, well, Inayatun brushed that off too. In a self-satisfied tone, she declared that she could give birth on her own, just like she had chosen whatever man she liked on her own and had gotten married on her own. 'As soon as you let out a wail, all of Cottonwood Grove will hear it, isn't that right, child? Your grandfather and grandmother will rush to our house, begging to hold you. And so will everyone else in this village. They will fight over who gets to carry you around,' Inayatun said to the baby in her stomach.

But Mat was less casual. Remembering the tale of his birth, which had so devastated his father—who had already gone astray while he was growing in his mother's belly, or so he'd been told—Mat Dawuk insisted on abstaining. He began to adamantly resist his wife's invitations to make love. Not because he didn't want to but because of the taboos that governed the behaviour of a father with a child in utero. He took more care when he was in the forest. He harvested only what he needed, tread gently on the earth and tried as hard as he could not to kill any living creature of any kind without a valid reason. He also tried to pray more regularly.

He had already promised Inayatun that he would never kill again, not for any reason. He would walk a bloody path no longer, that was partly why he had agreed to return home to Java. Even so, he couldn't instantly transform himself into a good person, at least not in the eyes of Cottonwood Grove. And it was difficult to rid himself of the bad habits shared by most migrant workers in Malaysia, who rarely prayed and disliked fasting. But his wife's pregnancy gave him a good reason to improve himself. Ignoring the curious and suspicious looks from the adults and children his presence elicited, he began showing up at the mosque for Friday prayers. Even though he didn't want to force his wife to join him there, he encouraged her to join him in praying more diligently at home. 'For the good of our unborn child,' that's what he said, like a model husband.

He took his old Quran out of its box, which had been stored away on a shelf. His Arabic wasn't too terrible, which surprised Inayatun a bit.

'I thought you said you couldn't read?' she asked.

'Not being able to read *Wiro Sableng* isn't the same thing as not being able to recite my prayers, now is it?'

'Where did you learn?'

'I'll tell you some other time.'

'What are you reading to our child?' she asked again.

'Surah Lukman,' Mat replied.

'Surah Lukman? For gratitude and obedience? Why not Surah Yusuf, for beauty?'

'No. I hope my child is devout and wise like Lukman, not all mixed up like its dad.'

'Or unruly like its mom,' Inayatun added, and they both quietly murmured Amen.

After that somewhat solemn moment passed, Inayatun returned to her first question, 'But you really don't want your child to be handsome like the Prophet Joseph?'

'How could I wish for a handsome child when I look like this?' Mat replied sheepishly.

'But its mother looks like this,' Inayatun grinned.

'So let it be your job to read the Surah Yusuf,' Mat said, sounding like an ulama proclaiming an edict.

'But what if I can't read Arabic?'

'Well, then, you won't be able to tell which is the Surah Lukman and which is the Surah Yusuf.'

'I could just pretend to know since I've heard people like my mother read it.'

'But you were certainly not pretending when you read the Divine Revelation in front of the Sub-district Head for the Independence Day ceremony in the village hall,' Mat said. 'You must have been about fourteen. You read Surah Ar Rahman, and your voice sounded so sweet every time you sang "*fabiayyi*".'

Inayatun stared. 'You know about that?'

Mat grinned. 'I already said I know everything about you.'

Inayatun was still stunned. She punched her husband's shoulder in irritation. 'Who are you really, Mat Dawuk?' Mat just smiled and let his wife punch him again.

'All right, so here's the Quran. But do your ablutions first. And put on your mukena.'

After that, they prayed together often. And, much to their surprise, they discovered that even something like that could be a source of happiness—at least, the kind of happiness that every family in Cottonwood Grove admired. And as the baby in Inayatun's belly grew, that feeling of joy grew and grew as well. But, as I said before, happiness is like a cup of coffee. A. Cup. Of. Coffee. And that's why it is sure to come to an...? An end!

Ah, my coffee has arrived. Praise Allah, does it smell good! This one is bound to be delicious, am I right, 'Ti? This is happiness. Ah, I should have married you long ago, 'Ti. Then we would certainly be happy. I'm sure of it.

A Grief That Cannot Be Sung

IF THERE WAS a song for the happiest part of the story, then we need a sad song for this part. Played softly and haltingly, audible and then silent, rising and falling, as the verses go on. It would have to be the saddest song ever written, if such a song exists. The strains of a viola played slowly and deeply might fit. Or a soulful wavering flute, that would be more suitable. Or one of those long, heartbreaking wails you hear in Bollywood films. But now that I've thought about it, it would be impossible for a song to capture this sadness—it simply couldn't. And sadness might not be the right word anyway. Maybe a better word would be tragedy, but this was no ordinary tragedy. So, none of the songs that tell of tragedy will hit the mark. That's it, I'm deciding: we don't need to sing at all.

But I think a lit cigarette would help set the atmosphere. Yes…that's exactly what I mean.

Before I go any further with the story, I have to say, in all honesty, that no one can truly know what happened that fateful day—except one person (I'll explain who he is later), and nobody believes him precisely because his story seems so convincing. So, what I'm going to tell you now is composed and collected from several different tales passed from one mouth to another; tales which hung in the air because no one snatched them down, because people chose to believe what they wanted to hear and not what they ought to hear; tales which slipped through the tears in woven bamboo walls, got stuck in the crevices of the fractured concrete mosque or lay cast aside and unclaimed by the roadside; stories which got trapped in the corners of a room, only shared from one person to another with the caveat that they must be guarded so that no one else would hear. Yes, that's how it is. What I can be sure of is that you are not going to find a tale that gets any closer to the truth than the tale I have to tell. You won't get it from the newspaper clippings published in the days after the incident, articles written hurriedly and carelessly by reporters who just wanted to finish their tasks and didn't do their best work. And you won't hear it from the respected folks around here—you all think they're incapable of speaking anything but the truth? Don't kid yourselves! And, of course, you won't hear it from the loudmouth know-it-alls in Cottonwood Grove!

So, the story goes...

That day, as usual, Mat went to the forest. About a month after the couple had come home, he and Inayatun had decided to become peasant farmers, cultivating forest land—the work that people of Cottonwood Grove had been doing for generations until most of them abandoned it to go overseas and work in Malaysia. In his plot, he had a few rows of corn, beans, several chilli pepper plants and different kinds of vegetables for them to eat or sell if it was a large harvest. During planting and weeding seasons, he would go to the forest in the morning, but once the plants didn't need as much tending, he would leave around midday just to check whether there was any damage from pests or raiding forest creatures and harvest any ripe vegetables. In the mornings, he would forage food for the goat, somewhere not too far from the house if possible. As much as he could, he avoided anything that would take him too far from the house or keep him away for too long so that he could spend more time with his pregnant wife.

But that day, he did, in fact, have to go to the forest. According to his calculations, it was time to pick the corn—the corn silk was darkening and beginning to wither, the tips of the husks were hardening and the cobs had begun to plump with soft young kernels. Around that time, the corn would be delicious no matter how it was cooked. It would be tasty in soup or a side dish, or grilled or roasted on a small spit. Steaming the stripped kernels and sprinkling them with dried coconut and salt would also be a treat. Plus, that day Inayatun had a special request; for the past few days, she had been asking for *kecacil*, the sour fruit of the gum-lac tree. 'I'm craving it,' she said. *Kecacil* were in season, but Mat knew the tree only grew deep in the forest.

'I'm heading out to the garden beds, In. You stay here at home,' Mat called out his goodbye, a sickle in his hand.

'Wait a minute!' Inayatun yelled from the kitchen and then appeared from inside the house with a shawl over her shoulders, a glass bottle filled with drinking water under her arm, and the small scythe that she usually used in the garden in her hand.

'Where are you going?' Mat asked, surprised.

'I'm going to join you in the forest,' Inayatun replied innocently. Mat looked displeased. His ugly face frowned.

'I can wait in the fields, choose the corn cobs that are ready to be twisted off, or pick the long beans while you look for the *kecacil* for me,' Inayatun went on, still with an innocent look on her face.

'Don't you know that even to reach the fields we have to walk quite a long way?' Mat admonished.

'If I get tired, you can carry me.' Now, Inayatun's innocent look broke out into a spoiled and mischievous smile. She put her arm around her husband's shoulders, with her hand still holding the small scythe.

Mat removed his wife's hand disapprovingly and shook his head firmly. 'Stay home!' he ordered, not wanting to be contradicted. Then, his expression unchanged, Mat wrapped his arms around his wife's body, picked her up, and carried her back inside. Inayatun resisted, but Mat knew how to overpower her.

Sitting Inayatun down on the only sofa in the house, Mat said, 'I'd be happy to carry you all around the forest—you don't have to ask twice, you don't have to be tired, I'll do it anytime you want. But later, after you give birth.'

'I don't like staying in the house all alone. And you'll surely be gone until afternoon,' Inayatun pouted with a quivering schoolgirl curve in her lip.

'I promise I'll only be gone a short while. I'll gather

just enough corn and beans, look for the *kecacil*, and come home straightaway,' Mat vowed.

'But what if Foreman Har comes again?' Inayatun blurted out, almost as if she hadn't intended to.

Mat's forehead wrinkled. 'Foreman Har came here? When?'

'Three days ago. In the morning, when you were out looking for goat feed.'

'On what business?'

'He asked about the forest land we work, what we had planted, whether you had already received our ration of hoes, whether we had enough albizia seeds or not, and things like that.'

'Well, isn't that his job?'

'If it was a professional matter, he should have met with you in the forest and not with me at the house.'

'Maybe he thought I was at home.'

'Maybe he already knew that you weren't at home, and that's precisely why he came.'

Mat was taken aback to hear his wife suggest such a thing. 'I don't like how he acts with me,' Inayatun continued.

'Well, what did he do?' Mat asked.

'He didn't do anything. Not yet.'

'Ah, you're just being oversensitive.'

'Maybe, but I know how men move, the look in their eyes. You know…'

'Enough.'

'He seemed to be looking for trouble. He said the land we are living on doesn't all belong to my father. A part of it is under Indonesian State Forest jurisdiction, so it belongs to the government. He said you should talk to the administrative office before the situation gets complicated.'

'Yes, I'll take care of it soon. Now, I have to go, otherwise I won't be home until late in the afternoon.'

Mat moved to leave, but Inayatun reached out and grabbed the hem of his shirt. 'Mat…' Inayatun looked strained. 'What if he comes again and tries to seduce me?'

Mat knew his wife. He understood her worry.

'I trust you.'

'But what if I betray your trust?'

'Then my child will guard it,' Mat said, caressing his wife's stomach.

'Mat, I'm really worried. Don't joke around.'

Mat fell silent, then gave a bitter little smile. 'If the child in your stomach cannot protect you, then maybe I can't keep my promise to you either.' That twisted smile grew more unpleasant as he continued, 'Or maybe two more people will wind up dead.'

'You'd kill us?'

'No, I'd kill him first, and then I'd kill myself.'

Sitting on the sofa, Inayatun threw her arms around her husband's waist and buried her face in his stomach. Then she lifted her face like a sulking child. 'So then let me come with you…'

Mat shook off his wife's embrace, stroked her hair, and tried to soothe her, while still showing his disapproval.

'Mat…'

'Stay at home.'

'It's not my wish; it's the wish of your unborn child!' Inayatun insisted.

'It's not good for pregnant women to talk nonsense.' Mat took Inayatun's cheeks in his hands, kissed her forehead and then the crown of her head. 'Stay at home,' he whispered, repeating his words, like an incantation.

When she couldn't move her body off the bed, she realized that her husband had indeed cast a spell on her.

'You'd better be careful with this stuff—if I'm paralysed now, your child will come out gape-mouthed and drooling!' Inayatun said in her final protest.

'That's fine. I'd happily lick the drool off my baby's face!' Mat replied lightly, retreating from their cozy shed and then closing the door.

'If you leave me like this, how will I be able to cook your dinner?' Inayatun yelled after him.

'As soon as I arrive at Pilang Pang Papat, the Four-Branched Tree, you'll be able to get down and move around,' Mat's voice could be heard replying from a distance.

Pilang Pang Papat, or the acacia tree with four large boughs, marked a resting place in the middle of the forest. The old tree used to have a wide canopy lush with leaves but had turned brittle with age, and some of its branches had withered. Still, a small spring with clear water, wide sparkling stones scattered across the bed of a trickling river, and shade from the surrounding trees made it a most comfortable place to rest for people returning from the forest after scavenging for firewood, foraging food for their animals, gathering teak leaves, or cultivating forest land like Mat was doing that day. Before so many from Cottonwood Grove had left for Malaysia, the place used to be lively, especially near afternoon when people were coming home from all directions of the forest, each shouldering a yoke, carrying the fruits of their labour.

In the time it took for him to smoke two cigarettes, Mat arrived there. He threw his cigarette butt into the rocks and stones in the roadside and smiled, imagining that right at that moment, back at the house, Inayatun was getting up off the day bed, cranky after being temporarily immobilized. If Inayatun's bad mood held until the afternoon, he thought, there might not be any dinner waiting for him when he got home.

'Where you going, Mat?' A voice called out the words of a friendly greeting but in an aggressive tone. Mat turned and saw a man in a green forest ranger uniform sitting casually on his dirt bike, which was leaning on its kickstand right under a large branch of the acacia tree. It was Foreman Hariyanto, who was usually called by his nickname, Foreman Har. This was the very man his wife had mentioned back at the house. His family had controlled the Cottonwood Grove forest for three generations. The son of Ranger Hartoyo and the grandson of Overseer Harjo, he was immediately recognizable, with his tall and robust build, his dark but handsome skin, and his brown-black hair—signs, it was said, of his mother's mother, who had mixed Ambonese and Spanish blood and came from a family who controlled the forests during the time of Dutch colonial power, ruling out of the large offices in what was then called the Rembang Residency.

'I'm going to my plot, sir,' Mat said, stopping and slowly turning around. The plot he meant was the piece of forest land worked by peasant farmers like him.

Foreman Har was only two or three years older than him, still, Mat replied with polite Javanese and called him 'sir'—from Foreman Har, men like Mat got permission to work the forest, received a ration of teak or albizia seeds to plant, hoes to break the earth and sometimes even a tiny quota of fertilizer, which was usually stale. In reality, the fact that the grandson of an Overseer had only risen to be a Foreman didn't automatically command much respect. But Mat chose to behave in a manner appropriate for a peasant towards a forest foreman.

'So, you aren't off to chop down trees?' Foreman Har asked. It was an accusatory joke.

'In the middle of the day?' Mat replied in a similarly joking tone.

'Oh, so you do it at night, eh?' Foreman Har continued. His grin widened, but his tone grew more threatening.

When they were both teenagers, Mat had knocked Hariyanto's teeth out after a prayer recitation in Centong village in a fight that had been one against four—and though a dozen years had passed, Mat was sure he could still break the guy's jaw with a single punch, but now wasn't a good time to do it. He had promised Inayatun he would return home quickly and didn't want any trouble. So, Mat lightly countered: 'I don't even have an axe, sir.'

'If I gave you a chainsaw, would you want to work as a logger, Mat?' Another voice posed the question; Hasan, who owned an unofficial lumber mill in Cottonwood Grove, appeared from the bushes behind a nearby tree. He was zipping up his fly, and his eyes shone with the relief of someone who had just taken a good leak.

'Interested, Mat?' Hasan, or as people called him, Woodsman Hasan, repeated his question, now standing next to Foreman Har's dirt bike. Hasan was about Mat's age, but as the son of Woodsman Hasim, the first man in Cottonwood Grove to own a chainsaw, he spoke with insufferable arrogance.

'Oh, no, 'San. I'll work my little plot,' Mat declined calmly, even though he knew the offer was no more than a taunt.

A state foreman socializing with an illegal logger in the middle of the forest was as ridiculous as a policeman conspiring with a thief in the lobby of the courthouse. Still, anyone who knew even a little bit about Cottonwood Grove and the forests that surrounded it would immediately get what was going on.

For hundreds of years, the lives of the people of Cottonwood Grove had depended on those forests, and after hundreds of years, they had learned to accommodate the bizarre behaviour of the creatures that inhabited it, both its invisible spirit guardians and the men in green uniforms who had kept control of it for generations. The intimacy between Foreman Har and Woodsman Hasan was inherited—their fathers, Ranger Hartoyo and Woodsman Hasim, weren't just friends; they were in-laws. Haryati, Ranger Hartoyo's oldest daughter and Hariyanto's older sister, was married to Hanan, Hasan's older brother. Hasan and Hariyanto had been friends since they were children. As teenagers, they frequented palm wine stalls. Together, they had experimented with and become addicted to painkillers back in the late eighties, when they were sold in the fishing port cities along the Javanese coast. Both were still known as regulars at the local whorehouses. They were both from the handful of families in Cottonwood Grove whose children didn't have to worry about finding a way to get to Malaysia to seek their fortune.

After a moment of silence, Hasan said, 'If I had a wife as pretty as yours, I'd be that way too, Mat. But I wouldn't just decline to go out and chop down trees; I wouldn't work the land either. I wouldn't work at all. I wouldn't leave the house, and in fact, I wouldn't even wear pants, just wrap a sarong around me from time to time. All I would do was lie in bed and cuddle. Just enjoy my privileges as a husband.' He laughed, slapping his thigh. 'Am I right, Foreman Har?'

Foreman Har guffawed. Mat was displeased with this line of conversation. He knew what kind of men he had before him. And, of course, he knew the story of the adolescent affair between Foreman Har and Inayatun. He remembered his conversation with Inayatun before leaving the house, but he didn't intend to make an issue out of it. He also postponed asking any questions about the issue of the Indonesian State Forest land, which he had planned to discuss with Foreman Har. He didn't want to lose his composure. Instead, pretending to smile, he took his leave. 'I'd better hurry. Otherwise I'll be in the fields until dusk. Excuse me, Mr Foreman. I'll be going, 'San.'

As he was walking away, Mat heard the revving motor of Foreman Har's dirt bike. When he looked over his shoulder, the bike had already disappeared, leaving only the growl of its engine fading into the distance, heading for the village. He kept walking and arrived at his plot of land about halfway through his fourth cigarette. Just as he had expected, the bright corn silk had begun to wither, and so the cobs were ready to be picked, at least to be boiled or grilled. The long beans could also be harvested. The row of red beans growing on the ridge weren't quite ripe, but their leaves, which were tasty steamed, were ready to be plucked.

Because his main goal in going to the forest was to look for *kecacil* fruit for Inayatun, he didn't waste any time. After making the rounds of his plot, righting cornstalks that had been knocked over by the wind and pulling weeds from between the red bean stems, he chose a few corncobs to bring home—ones that weren't too young, but not too old either.

As he plucked a cob from its stalk, Mat Dawuk felt a powerful twinge in his finger and yelled. The cob fell to the earth. Two scorpions came flying out from between the folds of its husk and went rolling in the dirt. One of these had dug its stinger into Mat's right pointer finger. His face flushed with shock and pain; clutching his stung finger, Mat lifted his foot to smash them, but remembering the baby in his wife's stomach, he quickly stopped himself and decided to just shoo the two poisonous creatures away.

Still massaging his finger, which was already quite red and swollen, Mat swallowed his rage and shook his head in disbelief. He also felt strangely unsettled; scorpions liked to make their home in cornhusks, so finding one there was nothing unusual, but the timing was. Scorpions usually appeared in the cornfields during the rainy season, and they liked the dry and 'clean' cornhusks the best. But these two had crouched in the folds of husks that were still green, and even though the sky had been cloudy the past few days, no rain had fallen yet.

As his swollen finger started to throb, he reminded himself that his main goal in coming to the forest had been to find *kecacil* for Inayatun. So, he satisfied himself with the young corn. Ten large ears would be enough for them to make whatever they wanted. He could leave the red bean leaf shoots for now—pluck them any other day. He would take only as many long beans as needed, just enough to be cooked along with the young corn. Just a tiny bundle was fine since the long beans had grown quite long. After that, he would head for the forest area where he could find the nearest gum-lac, which he was sure would be bearing fruit.

Hurrying a little, he grabbed a few sheaves of long beans and twisted them off the vines on the trellis. With his second tug, he felt a prick, small but startling, making him gasp once morc. This time, it was on the edge of his palm, right between his thumb and forefinger. It didn't hurt as much as the scorpion sting had, but the pang forced his left fist open, and all the long beans he had picked fell to the ground. Glancing at the wound on his hand, Mat found the culprit—the round head of a green whip snake, no bigger than the tip of his pinkie finger, was glaring up at him menacingly with bright yellow eyes. Its flat, sleek body was the same size and shade of green as the long beans, wound between the trellis and the vines. Not far away, another snake lay coiled.

So, the palm of his hand hadn't been pricked but bitten. He knew that the worst the snake's bite could do was make his hand itch, but it still vexed him. With his right pointer finger swollen and the palm of his left hand starting to tingle, Mat stood up straight, lifted his ugly face to the sky, and snorted in irritation. 'I'd rather have Foreman Har and Lumberjack Hasan gang up on me than get stung by scorpions and bitten by a whip snake.'

Before the words were even out of his mouth, Mat was surprised to hear himself grumbling to the forest about Foreman Har and Woodsman Hasan in the same breath as the two scorpions and two snakes. Woodsman Hasan's joke about his wife had made him move on quickly, like a cassette tape being fast-forwarded. Still, the man's voice now sounded again, as plainly audible as a radio speaker pressed to his ear, as clear as if Mat was watching those conceited lips move right before his eyes.

Then he thought of the revving dirt bike engine that had sounded the men's departure and the direction they had gone off in. Suddenly, he was worried.

He remembered Inayatun's words that morning, as she had insisted on joining him, and the baby growing in her stomach. And now he was terribly afraid.

Fear and shaking worry had long ago disappeared from his repertory of feelings, but now he felt them once again, only worse than he remembered—his heart pounded and his guts began to churn. His stomach was on fire. And it had nothing to do with the scorpions or the whip snake bite.

So, no longer bothering with the young corn that he

had harvested, the long beans he had just picked, or the *kecacil* fruit that he hadn't yet had a chance to gather, with no thought of the sickle he was still carrying, Mat turned and set off sprinting along the pathway home. As his heartbeat raced faster and faster, out of control, he quickened his pace and lengthened his stride almost as if he was flying—no, it wasn't *as if,* he truly flew.

But no matter how swiftly a mother bird can soar, she still can't catch the egg that is falling from her nest. And it was thus for Mat. No matter how fast he ran or flew back to his house, not even if he had been as powerful as Brama Kumbara—remember the freedom fighter from the old TV show?—he wouldn't have had the strength to deflect this stroke of fate, which was to put an end to his happy life with Inayatun—or, more accurately, which was to put an end to his life, period.

He arrived at the cow shed at the exact moment—he couldn't have been more precise—at the *exact moment* disaster struck.

Everything Ashen

In earlier times, when the western sky was turning purple and day was turning into dusk, the trees around the cow shed at the forest's edge were usually clamorous with the calls of finches flying home to their nests. The gently whistling breeze would occasionally gust into a brisker wind, turning all the trees into a rippling ocean of rustling leaves, this harmonious orchestra only punctuated by the staccato of a twig cracking or branch creaking in the distance. The cry of a mother ape calling her children to climb into their nest in some far corner of the jungle, or the steps of a pair of deer delicately making their way towards their resting place in a cluster of bushes, was accompanied by the rattle of night insects greeting darkness and its blessings. All this signalled a time as perfect as possible for the people who were just returning home from the forest to rest for a moment before washing off the day's dirt. The softly lilting prayers and poetry descending from the mosque rooftops in the middle of the village confirmed that God was still steadfast in his dominion, changing night for the day before bringing back the morning—just as was said of Him many times in the holy book. Humans had no choice but to mull over how small and insignificant they were, powerless creatures made for no other reason than to worship Him.

But not that afternoon.

That afternoon was different. Totally different. There were no chirping finches. The wind choked; the air was still. There were no rustling leaves, cracking branches, or swaying boughs. It was as if the monkeys were trapped in their hideouts, the deer hobbled, and the night insects gone mute. The sky was silent.

The only sound that could be heard was a long, deafening whine: '*Ngingingingingin*g!'

Nothing but *nging*! But could that be called a sound? Could hearing a sound like that even be called hearing?

Because if so, then at the same time, it could be said that eyes are still seeing, even when all they see is the colour of ash. A grey greyer than the meaning of the word grey itself.

Grey, grey as ashes.

There was no colour besides that. Not the thick blackish-red seeping from the gaping wound in Inayatun's stomach as she lay there in his arms. Not the thick blackish red smeared across his cheek and drenching his tattered clothes. Not the thick blackish-red that seemed to be spreading everywhere.

Everything was ashen.

Is it accurate to say that his chest, his hands and feet, could still feel if the only thing they could feel was the limp body of his wife, growing heavier and heavier in his embrace? Because truthfully, throughout his entire body, across every inch of his skin, there was nothing but a sensation of weightlessness.

No, it was not because he had run so fast that he practically flew, or actually flew, his body covered in his wife's blood as he carried her in his arms from the cow shed at the edge of the Cottonwood Grove forest to the community health centre in Galeng Gede, which was at least fifteen minutes away, if one was riding an RX Special motorbike speeding over forty kilometres an hour. He thought that his body must have felt that way because he was no longer made of flesh and blood—his muscles and bones must have dissolved, leaving nothing but skin encasing a gaping cavity. There was nothing.

Empty. Void. Hollow.

Ridden with holes.

As light as straw. Dry straw.

Like an insubstantial wisp of cotton that flies and floats wherever the wind carries it. Weightless. Whisked away.

And *nging*...

His body was empty, his head was empty. He certainly didn't realize, as he raced along the Cottonwood Grove village road, that women and children were screaming, running, scattering in terror. How could they not, when the sight was worse than anything they had ever seen, worse than even the most horrifying scenes in *Battle with the Red Devil*, which they had watched on the eve of Independence Day at the outdoor screening on the village administration office's front lawn? It may have been that he was aware of nothing except his wife's condition when he banged on the door of the community health centre's emergency room, howling down the corridor for the doctor.

'Help my wife! Help! Help my child! Help! Help!'

The words didn't come out like a bark or bellow but a final plea for mercy. They didn't even sound as if he expected help but like the only words left to a man who no longer knew what else to say.

Even so, they were more than enough to startle the doctor and nurses on call in the small, sub-district community health centre. They had cared for patients as badly off, but this was different. They didn't need some tale-telling troublemaker to persuade them that standing before them was a murderer carrying his victim—to deceive the authorities, maybe, or because he was criminally insane. They didn't need to hear the whole story about Mat Dawuk—and the dozens of people whose souls he had supposedly obliterated—to feel shocked and afraid. His hideous face, smeared with blood, was enough to convince them he would slaughter everyone in the place.

And how pale was the doctor's face as, with all the trembling courage he could muster, he had to say that neither the victim nor the baby in her belly could be saved.

'You…your wife…is…gone,' the doctor stammered. 'And…and so is the baby.'

The doctor had steeled himself, certain that those bloodstained hands would grab for the collar of his white coat, close around his neck, or crush his skull. So he was surprised when the maniac only shook his head in confusion, eyes hollow, and asked, in an almost inaudible voice: 'Gone?'

'Yes. Your wife and child…are gone.' This time, the doctor spoke more fluidly, though he was still shaking.

Mat Dawuk remained dumbfounded. People who had heard of his ferocity and cold heart, even if they had witnessed him in that state, wouldn't have believed it. This clearly wasn't Mat Dawuk—or at least, it wasn't the Mat Dawuk they had understood him to be.

'Gone.' He repeated the word as if it were completely foreign and difficult to pronounce. He had never received an education, had never cracked open even a primary school workbook, and couldn't read any of the *Wiro Sableng* series that he had collected, but surely it was impossible that he had never heard the word 'gone'.

He was well-acquainted with death. His mother had died giving birth to him. His grandfather, the person who loved him most in the world, had left him, vanished and was presumed dead when he was only five years old. He had witnessed the death of his depraved father, who hated him, after his body had been flattened by an *Indonesia* bus on the Semarang-Surabaya route just as he stepped out of his favourite palm wine stall. Of course, there were also the people Mat Dawuk had killed. And there was his own soul—Mat Dawuk himself had survived numerous brushes with death. But all of that had just been called 'death', maybe that's why he hadn't often heard the word 'gone' and needed some time to process it.

'Gone,' he murmured again, like an elementary school student trying to sound out a difficult word.

'Will you take your wife home?' the doctor asked. 'Or should we prepare the body here?'

As if he hadn't heard, without displaying any of the appropriate reactions of a husband who had just lost his wife—like a grimace of shock or a wail of lament—he only gaped, then looked away, up at the open sky, as if seeking an answer. He looked at the clouds gathering, and that blackness was the first colour he could see that afternoon since everything had gone grey. He watched the rolling coils growing thicker and broader, ushering in a rising wind—the first breath of air he felt. There were a few isolated rumbles of thunder. The first was small, followed by a flash of lightning, louder booms rang out, and finally, the loudest. Those were the first sounds he was able to hear besides '*nging*'—and that confounding word, 'gone'. But he still couldn't resolve his incomprehension, or explain his sense of emptiness as the word hung in the air.

Another clap of thunder. He raised his blood-streaked face. The strong wind had brought the rain along with it, and thick drops were already pounding the health centre's asbestos roof. But Mat Dawuk walked out into the yard, looking straight up at the sky as if the rain would finally help him understand.

Then came a loud rumble from another direction. He turned his gaze from the sky to the gate of the health centre behind him. Through his blood-matted, rain-soaked hair, he saw a group of five or six people jumping down off their motorbikes. They were followed by more motorbikes and more people. Then a pickup arrived and even more people leapt down.

'That's Mat Dawuk!' Someone shouted his name, but not to get his attention. 'He's the one who killed Inayatun and Foreman Har!' someone else called out, louder than the rain, which was now roaring.

But it didn't seem to register. His expression hadn't changed since the doctor had first told him that his wife and child were 'gone'. Still dumbfounded. Empty. He was still seeking an explanation for his inexplicable feelings.

Then the slurs and insults came, hurled down upon him like rain. Followed by: 'Kill Mat Dawuk!'

Then: 'Yeah, kill him!' And then: 'Crush him!' And, 'Burn him!' 'Murder him!' 'Murder him!' 'Murder him!' 'Slaughter him!' 'Slit his throat!'

And Mat Dawuk was still standing there, bewildered, when a bamboo pole as thick as his thigh struck the nape of his neck, on the right. His head bounced to the side, he swayed, his knees buckled, and he staggered but didn't fall. His head turned unhurriedly towards the blow, like someone looking to check whether a leaf had just fallen onto his shoulder, then looked up again. The afternoon sky was blackening. The rain kept roaring. The whole world had gone ashen. Even so, as the crowd behind him pressed closer, thundering their insults and threats, holding their weapons at the ready, Mat Dawuk caught a glimpse of Woodsman Hasan in the crowd. He squinted as if trying to reassure himself that the man who was now yelling the loudest, hurling the most vicious insults, was the same man who had earlier lunged at him but missed, instead splitting open the chest of his friend, Foreman Har, with his very own hatchet, and then scrambling away.

Mat Dawuk fixed Woodsman Hasan with a piercing look—but then came another blow, and another, this time with a plank of wood as big as a horse carriage axle, slammed into the nape of his neck. The force of the impact split the wood in two. Still, his gaze didn't falter, and Mat Dawuk continued to glare a warning at Woodsman Hasan.

Then, a metal pipe slammed straight down onto his skull. The crowbar buckled, and the rain splattering from Mat Dawuk's long curly hair mixed with fresh blood from his split scalp. His eyelids shrunk back in surprise. His shoulders slumped, his body went limp, and then he fell headlong.

'Finish him!'

'Slaughter him!'

'Slit his throat!'

Then rods of bamboo, wooden planks, stones and kicks and punches, weapons blunt and sharpened, now one at a time, now all together, descended upon him.

The rain kept falling and falling, like water that an angry father pours over a son who hasn't roused for pre-dawn prayers. Maghrib fell with a dusk far darker than usual. The muezzin's trembling voice broke into a hoarse and reluctant cough. The people, of whom there were dozens, surged over Mat Dawuk's limp body like a flood that gushes out of a clogged ditch: thick and black, full of garbage, full of rage.

Hmmm…that's enough.

Or at least that's enough for now—time for intermission, as the Bollywood films say. My coffee is finished. And you've smoked all your cigarettes, haven't you? I want to go home. I'm sleepy. I didn't sleep at all last night. I'm hungry, too. I'll continue tomorrow—if I'm still alive.

'So, What Happened to Mat?'

HE WAS THERE the next day, just as he had promised, on the same sofa he had been sitting on the day before, the whole morning and into midday, telling stories; first passionate and absorbed, then distracted and almost ambivalent, then just stopping whenever he pleased—leaving us, his audience, dumbfounded, throwing down our empty packs of cigarettes, stirring the grounds in our coffee cups and cursing him, almost in synchrony: 'That damned Warto!'

The only thing different from the day before was his appearance.

This morning, he walked into the *warung* wearing a sarong the way it was supposed to be worn—it could even be said, neatly. His clothes were more or less clean, and his face radiated self-confidence, like those retired men who go out for a stroll in the early morning, greeting their neighbours before saying their dawn prayers and reciting a sufficient bit of the Quran. He didn't have to try as hard to get attention as he had the day before and immediately found himself at the centre of a crowd, snatching up whatever cup of coffee he could get his hands on and grabbing all the packs of cigarettes tossed onto the table.

Clearly, he had gotten what he needed. But he still seemed to have a problem. A few people in the crowd, who had listened to his story along with me, repeated their complaints of the previous day, venting their pent-up annoyance, hurling insults and lodging accusations and voicing scepticism about whether the story we were being told had actually happened. Did Warto Kemplung know the story? And if he knew the story, was he telling it truthfully? And if he really knew the story and was telling it as truthfully as he could, then why did it seem that certain parts of it didn't make any sense? How could he know what Mat and Inayatun had said to each other in their cozy shed? How could he know how Mat felt when his wife died? Who was he, truly? Was he himself Mat Dawuk?

Warto smiled condescendingly at those accusations.

'So let's say, for example, that Teacher Tarmidi tells his students about a terrified mouse-deer whose heart is pounding as it tiptoes slowly past a snoring tiger. Would he first have to ask the little deer how it would feel if it came across a tiger? Or, to recount how soundly the tiger was sleeping, what a beautiful dream it was having, would Teacher Tarmidi have to first become a tiger himself?' he mocked, belligerent.

It didn't seem like anyone had an answer. Maybe they didn't understand what he was asking. But that was just fine by Warto Kemplung, who had posed the question so he could answer it himself.

'Of course, I have to forgive the pathetic workings of

dry and barren souls such as yours,' he continued, growing more scathing, more impassioned, like a teacher scolding an entire class who had failed their exam. 'But someone who doesn't understand how beautiful a tale or story can be, how moving a myth or legend, is truly unfortunate.' He shook his head, his expression suffused with pity.

And he wasn't finished yet.

'Ah, of course, this is what you get.' He shook his head again. 'This is what happens when people go to the shadow puppet show just for the action; watch *ketoprak* theatre just for the slapstick jokes; watch *ludruk* just to see how pretty the lady boys are; listen to radio dramas without suspecting that sometimes heathens pretend to be kings or warriors just to destroy their children's faith and morals!' He turned away and tossed the butt of his cigarette—a cigarette he had pilfered from someone.

'But come on, you are truly stringing us along, 'Plung!' someone from the crowd broke in, his finger pointing in accusation, his face hostile. 'You brag and crow about how you're here to tell a bloody tale. So where is it? Bloody tale, bloody hell! You've finished how many cups of coffee, stolen all our cigarettes, and your story is just going in circles. You're even forcing us to listen to your Bollywood serenades! There's no clear point to any of it!'

Warto Kemplung welcomed that accusation with a disdainful smile. 'So, you all want a more straightforward story?' He paused for a minute, then continued, 'Well, all right then. If that's how you want it, you might as well just swallow the lies you've been fed by the people of Cottonwood Grove: Mat Dawuk killed his wife and

Foreman Har, and then Woodsman Hasan, and then he fled, and after almost fifteen years, he returned, and then he was beaten and burned alive. End of story!' He smacked the bamboo couch that he was sitting on. The full cups trembled in their saucers while the empties and packs of cigarettes gave a little jump.

Warto Kemplung was enraged. But, if you scrutinized him, it might be more accurate to say he *looked* mad than he really *was* mad. It was as if he wanted the attention and something more—he wanted respect, or at least that's what I suspected, and, in the end, of course, a few more cups of coffee and some smokes to go along with them.

It was clear; that was why he had cut off his story at the precise moment that his listeners wanted him to keep going. He had cunningly kept the critical event to himself. He must have been purposefully stalling, or maybe he would never really bring it forth. This man understood, or at least appeared to understand, the matter of suspense. He was like Scheherezade in the 1001 Nights. And if the captive princess was going to live, this big talker would need more coffee and cigarettes.

Yup, this is how it was. I was the unfortunate—and stupid—king, willing to come to this coffee shop early in the morning, setting aside my duty to report on unimportant events to listen to a bullshitter tell a story that was potentially even more unimportant and—it was painfully clear—in no way guaranteed to be true.

I edged closer, as the tension from Warto Kemplung's feigned rage still buzzed in the air. The people were quiet, but I was sure that it wasn't because they felt guilty, as

Warto might have been hoping. To me they seemed annoyed, just as I myself secretly felt. They were only demanding their rights: they wanted to hear the bloody tale Warto had promised them, but instead Warto had mocked them as rubes who didn't understand the art of storytelling.

On Warto's face, the contrived anger faded and what remained was the awkward dismay of a health tonic seller who had put off a potential buyer. Then, he seemed to be trying to recover the situation.

'Okay then. So…that's how it was. In the end, Mat Dawuk…'

When his gaze did not meet the curious faces he was so desperately seeking at that point, Warto Kemplung stopped the next chapter of his story short. He looked around again, to the left and right, searching, still trying to scavenge one last buyer of his gibberish, but he didn't find any. He waited another moment, and when there was still no response, he furtively, almost delicately, pulled his sarong up over his head, and then with the same delicacy, began to move his ass off the couch he had been sitting on.

This was dire. I could not let it be. Before it was too late, before he truly stood up and left, which would mean that I wouldn't get what I was looking for, with full premeditation, I thrust a Dji Sam Soe clove cigarette into my mouth and then threw the pack—which, of course, was still full—down right in front of him.

'Cigarette, Pak Warto?' I offered, lighting the cigarette in my mouth, then placing a lighter atop the sweetly positioned pack.

He sat back down. His eyes, just as I had hoped, were drawn to the cigarettes and lighter. I knew he wanted a smoke, but what was also cheering him up, and I could see it on his face, was that now he had the attention he craved.

'Well, hey, you don't need to put yourself out,' he said, summoning his good manners.

I let the smoke slowly pool out of my mouth and played with it a bit, showing him how delicious it was before giving him a smile as a sign of encouragement. 'It's nothing, sir. Please.'

'Well, all right, if you insist. It's not good to refuse a bit of good fortune, now is it?' he said quickly and just as quickly his hand had slipped one cigarette between his lips and another behind his ear, exactly as I had seen him do the day before.

'Wow, this is a Cricket lighter. Do you have family that went to Malaysia, brother? Or maybe you've been there?' he asked, still making small talk. He weighed the lighter in his hand. 'This is pretty nice, brother. It must have been expensive.'

'Not really, sir. It wasn't expensive. Plenty of them are sold in Indonesia nowadays,' I replied. Then, acting as if it had just occurred to me, I asked: 'Oh, by the way, have you already had some coffee, sir?'

His gleeful but shy smile showed he wanted some.

'Coffee! Two!' I shouted. 'One sweet. And for you, Pak Warto?'

'The usual!'

I smiled.

Waiting for the coffee, we both were silent. I observed

the flashy and fast way he smoked, noting how much he enjoyed it. It didn't take long before the cigarette between his lips was twice as short as the one between mine. I had been watching him smoke since I first saw him, but I still didn't understand how it could go that quickly. At the moment I thought was right, I asked the question I had prepared before I even arrived that morning: 'So, what happened to Mat, sir?'

He pulled the much-shortened cigarette from his lips and gasped happily. 'So you were listening too, is that right?'

'I came here early this morning just to hear the rest of the story, sir,' I said, a bit flustered.

He grinned. 'Let's wait until the coffee arrives.'

Cottonwood Grove

COTTONWOOD GROVE IS a place where people try to solve every problem atop a mattress—and those that can't be solved are quietly shoved under a pillow.

Who knows how a grove of cottonwoods grew in the middle of a teak forest?

And, if you think about it, isn't it strange that there were people, village ancestors, who decided to live there, clear the forest, and name the place Cottonwood Grove?

It's downright astonishing. First, the place was almost equidistant from the Java Sea to the north and the Solo River in the south, stuck right in the middle. On top of that, there was nothing special about the place. There was no large spring, which usually draws people to stop and settle; there were only stagnant ponds, which became nothing but mud wallows in the dry season. The land there, just like the forest in northern Java, was hard. Its fertility was depleted after only five planting seasons, trying the patience of all who worked it. They couldn't be fishermen because they were too far from the sea, but they also couldn't be called farmers, not like their neighbours in the southern forests, whose abundant river waters replenished their fertile soil every year. Because of that, they had just been peasants working the forest land for generations. 'Contract workers', that's what they called themselves. Not surprisingly, they became lackeys of the Great Sultan when the Javanese still reigned triumphant. Then they became coolies for the ruling class during the Company era. Then they took orders from the men in green uniforms, even after the country was independent, before finally leaving to haul rocks for Malaysians.

Was there indeed ever a grove of cottonwood there? And if there was, what, in fact, can be done with a cluster of cottonwood trees, such that one would be a reason to live there? I don't understand it, and I also don't believe it. I have never encountered even one cottonwood stump, let alone a tree that was still growing. And it's been a very long time since the people of Cottonwood Grove had enough cotton to stuff their mattresses or pillows.

So, if it wasn't because of the cottonwood, was it because of the teak? Ah, but that doesn't make any sense either!

Javanese teak is, without a doubt, the best wood in the world; that is now indisputable. If the buildings in heaven use wooden sills, then those sills are made from Javanese teak. But for some reason, neither the Javanese, and certainly not their lowly woodcutters, have ever gotten any blessings from their teak forests—they haven't gotten any in the past, they're not getting any now, and they never will get any, not until the last teak tree is chopped down. In fact, it's the opposite. For hundreds of years, they have suffered because of it. Not long after that infamous ancient warrior Mur Jangkung stepped onto Javanese soil, The Company discovered the best thing to steal from this land, and it was teak wood. When Ndoro Tuwan Guntur arrived and opened the Great Anyer-Panarukan Post Road, they chopped down teak for this and that. Sugarcane factories were built, and teak was harvested once more for fuel. It was that way, too, when The Government infested Java with its railway. The railway was made out of iron, but of course, the ties and crossties were teak. And all that time, for hundreds of years, for generations, from their great-great-grandfathers down to their great-great-grandchildren, the Javanese people, and especially the people of Cottonwood Grove, were nothing but woodcutters. And for this, they received only half of what the buffalo they drove to drag the logs from the middle of the jungle to the side of the main road or the northern dockyards full of ships, from Gresik to Sedayu and Jepara, got—but, sharing the fate with those buffalo, they were just as mercilessly whipped!

So, maybe another old story just might be true: the story that was never acknowledged—even fiercely denied—by the people of Cottonwood Grove themselves. Their ancestors weren't wandering adventurers who came looking for a place to live, cleared the jungle, planted crops, and bred there. No. They were exiles. Or, more precisely, a pair of exiles who had been banished and cursed.

Have you heard the tale? Aha…of course, not. When would they ever tell it to you?

Long ago, in some religious boarding school somewhere, a virtuous and humble *kyai* had a daughter who was beautiful but wild and hopelessly lazy. His daughter's stubborn impertinence made the *kyai* nervous, and he wanted to marry her off to the son of a *kyai* from a bigger religious school. But the daughter refused to accept the arrangement. She had no interest in being a housewife. She was just happy to play and joke around with the other girls her age. On the day the young man's people were set to visit to arrange a proposal, the girl was busy sewing on the veranda of her father's prayer house with her friends. It just so happened that the needle she was using in her handiwork slipped from her fingers. The prayer house veranda was elevated like a stage, supported by tall wooden stakes, and the space beneath it was used as a cattle pen. The needle fell through a crack in the floorboards onto the ground. She considered going down there but couldn't be bothered. Her playmates wanted to help her retrieve it, but she forbade them. She remembered that the youth who was set to marry her was arriving that day and would certainly have to walk across the veranda. And she wanted to know whether this young man would be helpful to her or not.

'Ah, let it be. Someone will certainly fetch it for me. And whoever he is, if he is indeed a man, I will marry him,' she said.

Not long after, a young man climbed up the veranda steps, holding out the needle that the girl had dropped. But he wasn't the *kyai*'s son who came to ask for her hand—he was an ugly young Kalang from the labouring caste with coarse dark skin, who usually came to bring firewood and feed for the animals, occasionally joining in prayer. Kalang people were practically untouchable, rumoured to be the descendants of a long-ago union between a woman and a monkey, good for hauling stones to build temples and not much else. Still, a promise had been made, and it could not be taken back. So, the *kyai*'s young daughter chose the young Kalang for her husband.

The *kyai* was furious and ashamed. Instead of blessing the couple, he banished them—telling them to go far away, so far that he would never have to see their faces again. And he did not forget to curse them. He cursed his daughter thus: the girl, and all her daughters and granddaughters, would never be able to restrain themselves or remain faithful to the men they had chosen for their husbands, just as her father had not been able to restrain her. To the young Kalang, he decreed that his expert knowledge of the field, forest, livestock and such matters would still never be enough to support his wife and children.

Then, bearing those curses, the pair set out on their journey. Deep in the forest, far from the north and almost unreachable from the south, with eastern and western limits so distant they could not be imagined, they decided to stop and stay and start a family. And once the place grew busy and bustling, it was named Cottonwood Grove.

And that's how it was…

But you must remember, brother, this is a fairytale, so don't think about it too hard. Go ahead, drink your coffee. I know, educated people who work in an office like yourself here must recognize this story, right? It's so similar to other fairytales it must be a made-up tale, that's what you think, right? I beg you to understand that this is a story told by a humble man from little old Cottonwood

Grove. Such is the quality. But aren't stories always born from the stories that came before?

I'll take another cigarette, yes? Thank you. I'll continue.

As I said before, even though this story has been passed down for generations in Cottonwood Grove, at the end of the story the grandfathers will always tell their grandchildren, or the fathers who are telling their children will say, and of course, in all earnestness, 'This is just a story, so you don't have to believe it.'

And that's what the people of Cottonwood Grove have done for the entirety of their history: they have refused to believe the story of their origins.

Do you know how the people of Cottonwood Grove reject the truth of this story? First, they boast about their skin, which is, on average, lighter than those of the people from the surrounding villages. With that light skin, they can protest: how could the people of Cottonwood Grove have descended from a dark Kalang?

It makes sense, doesn't it? Maybe at first glance, but we can easily refute such an argument. What's strange about their light skin? Here is the reasoning. Perhaps it's true that the *kyai*'s daughter married that young Kalang, the firewood hauler. But, remember the curse—it also could be that the forefather of the people of Cottonwood Grove is not in fact that young Kalang. Confused? Look around the village. You'll find that many of the children here look more like their father's brother or their friend's father than their dad.

Second, they always boast about their piety. 'Coastal people are often religious, that's nothing unusual. But for peasant farmers to be devout, now that's truly extraordinary,' that's how they always pat their backs. And sure, that cannot be denied. There are no mosques more prosperous than those here.

Their children can fluently recite their *a-ba-ta-tsa* as soon as they can talk. Their prayer recitation is excellent, their devotional poetry sweet and melodious. They diligently pray five times a day, bowing their heads to the earth, and their *tahajud* and *rawatib* prayers are in order, too. But isn't the flesh of the watermelon quite a different colour than its skin? It's the same thing here; it turns out that the smooth-skinned June plum is craggy on the inside, am I right?

You must have heard the old jokey adage: 'The faith is strong, but the will is weak.' That's the people of Cottonwood Grove. Over time, from era to era, the people here have always a problem with the business. Yeah, I mean *that* business. They redouble their prayers, hoping that will keep them far from sinful behaviour. Unsurprisingly, those people know their verse, and they understand its guidance. It is God the almighty who guards His humble servants, but they forget, the one who has the responsibility to guard a humble servant above all is the servant himself, right? If it's not yours, you have no right to it. You can't trust in God without also making an effort. If it's rotten at the core, then in the end your faith won't be strong enough to fight temptation.

So you know, my brother, before the era of cell phones, the stories of sleeping around in Cottonwood Grove were quite funny—I'm just going to whisper this part since

I'm only telling you. Now, all you need to do is push the button with the picture of the little green telephone, and you can talk straightaway.

Hello, hello, hello, it's set. Or just tap-tap-tap, beep-boop-beep-boop, where should we meet up, done. Before, it wasn't so easy. But that doesn't mean that it was so difficult either.

If in the fields, let's say, a pair of lovers—who, of course, were not husband and wife—could make an arrangement just by placing a hoe in a particular spot with the handle pointing upwards. If possible, they would do their business right there. *Cak-cek*! If it was a little more complicated, they would meet at night, at a place they had agreed upon, arranged, of course, through mutually understood signals. And mind you, that didn't rule out the house of one of the parties. If the situation was somewhat accommodating, the back door or window could be left open, and the sweetheart came in. But if that was impossible, and meeting somewhere else was dangerous because it might invite attention, then a slit in the kitchen's bamboo wall would suffice. Not seeing each other's faces or touching each other's bodies was fine; the important thing was the stick found its hole. That part still felt just the same. Short and sweet was no big deal either; after all, they could always do it again another night.

A rendezvous in the forest in general was easier and more enjoyable. It was enough to drive a sickle or an axe blade into a tree branch, which was the invitation to make love. Unlike the fields, which were more exposed, the shady forest made it easier for a tryst to be immediately carried out to fruition right there on the spot. Even a small bush, as long as the leaves had grown in lush, could serve as a love nest. The bed depended on what was around—a baby sling belonging to the female lovebird was most often used. But, if there wasn't one of those, it wasn't necessary to make a fuss trying to find something else. The forest floor, especially if it was the rainy season, was padded enough for a naked backside being hounded by lust. If you wanted even more fun, you might look for a bush near a teak tree. The piles of withered and fallen teak leaves were quite soft, clean, and just a little bit slick. So, while lovemaking, you could also slip and slide.

If you want to know how it feels, go ahead and try it, but if you ask me, why bother? The thing is, now, the teak trees have all been chopped down by Indonesian State Forest Enterprise, Perhutani, and the albizia trees have taken their place. And from the looks of them, tall and spindly albizias aren't comfy for romance.

Returning to the people of Cottonwood Grove's origin story, not so long ago, they found a new way to refute it. Soon after the '87 General Election, after Golkar won its first-ever victory in the village, the price of petroleum was rising, while the coastal factories were using less and less firewood to smoke their fish. At the same time, the green-uniformed forest security forces were growing more aggressive with the woodcutters—except of course, the ones willing to team up with them. So, the people of Cottonwood Grove began to abandon their fields in droves, disobeying sacred taboos against leaving the land of their birth. Following those from surrounding villages, they began crossing to Malaysia.

But this was funny too: once they had left the forest of their homeland, it turns out they wound up working in another country's forest. In fact, they ended up living in a forest they didn't know at all, with trees they didn't know the names of, sleeping in thickets with their hearts pounding—not because they were with their next-door neighbour's wife, but because they were being chased by the Royal Police and civilian troops. But, after three election cycles, they could demonstrate that they weren't the same Cottonwood Grove folk they had been before, and the new Cottonwood Grove was no longer the old Cottonwood Grove people knew. Thanks to Malaysia, the men of Cottonwood Grove were now nothing like the young cursed Kalang. Now, they were able to amply support their wives and children.

But could this disprove the old origin story, that they were the descendants of a pair of cursed exiles, or did it give it more credence? *Wallahu a'lam bissawab*. Only Allah knows the truth.

Anyway, like I said before, this is just a story, just a legend that might borrow a bit from other pre-existing legends. So you don't have to believe it. But if you ask me, I will say: I believe it.

Mat Dawuk is Dead!

AH, SO IT turns out you all are listening in! How nice for you! It's no longer the era of radio plays, you know? You listen, you pay! Cough up some cigarettes!

Oh, no, that's plenty from you, my brother. This is more than enough. Don't go through any trouble. Your cigarettes are of good quality, put them in your pocket. If you put them down just anywhere, they'll get snatched up by demon hands. Your lighter, too, my brother. This is a nice lighter, I beg you to keep an eye on it.

Good. So, you still want to know what happened to Mat Dawuk, right…? He died.

Yes, he died. That's what you think happened, right?

And you all know, that's what the people of Cottonwood Grove wanted. Mat Dawuk, dead! That's what they thought should have happened.

In front of the Galeng Gede Community Health Centre, all of the weapons, the sharp ones and the rusty ones, had all been wielded; they had hurled and pounded stones, large and small; they had swung bamboo rods, yoke poles, hoe handles, carriage axles, table legs, splintered chairs, broken bits of fences, the backs of hospital benches. There is no expression more accurate to describe Mat Dawuk's body when the policemen who came too late dragged him from the melee and threw him into the back of the patrol pickup than *nggepeng ilir*, flattened like a fan. The throng regretted that they had not gone farther by hacking that bastard to bits and hurling his remains into the swirling swollen waters of the nearby ditch to let the flood carry them away—but, even so, Mat Dawuk should have been dead because Mat Dawuk deserved to die.

He had viciously murdered Inayatun and Foreman Har. Whatever had led up to that, he should have died; the people of Cottonwood Grove were sure of it, and parents would say as much to their children later when they were forced to tell the tale. They didn't care all that much that the first and only witness to the murder was Woodsman Hasan, who, on an average day and in all kinds of matters, was unreliable, and whose testimony had come from a mouth still stinking of palm wine and gasping for breath.

They also didn't trouble themselves with the police's findings: that stuck in the gash in Foreman Har's chest was a hatchet everyone knew belonged to Woodsman Hasan.

But if you all want to know what the people of Cottonwood Grove were thinking, what they didn't have to say to one another because they all already knew, and what they would keep to themselves and leave out of the stories they would tell their descendants, then listen up:

It was right for Mat Dawuk to die because he had to die, somehow. Even if, on that afternoon, there had been no one who came running, gasping for breath in between his screams to Allah that Mat Dawuk had just slaughtered his own wife because she had been sleeping with Foreman Har, Mat Dawuk would have still had to die. Even if he had never killed one mosquito, one single, measly mosquito!

Know why? Mat Dawuk had to die because he was an ugly man who had married the most beautiful woman ever born in Cottonwood Grove, because that unlikely and peculiar couple—that unimaginable love—reminded them of the legend of Siti, the *kyai*'s daughter and Suta, the young Kalang, the ancestors they had always refused to acknowledge. They didn't want the tale that they would have preferred was long forgotten to be spun again. They didn't like the curse they kept on trying to escape to be brought back to life—especially not in a way that was so obvious, clear as day. They could not accept it!

Mat Dawuk had to die. *He had to*. And because they hadn't yet found a better time than that afternoon in front of the community health centre, in the pouring rain, they had to seize the opportunity—otherwise, they would be sorry.

And indeed, they should be sorry.

Just Before the Call to Prayer

On the seventh day after that bloody afternoon, at least half the men in Cottonwood Grove were neatly dressed and perfumed long before the call to Maghrib prayers filled the air. In their houses, they each had put on their best sarong, rarely worn button-down shirts or brightly coloured Melayu clothes, gifts from family who had returned home from the neighbouring countries. It was inappropriate for people getting ready for a memorial service, and only more so since it would soon be the first night of Ramadan. But who cared?

If you want honesty, there wasn't a noticeable atmosphere of mourning in Cottonwood Grove that afternoon. It was true that two of their residents had been killed seven days ago. But, at the same time, the villainous murderer had been punished, so the overall sense was that there was nothing to mourn about, right? After Maghrib prayers were done, the people would hustle out to one of the two houses that were holding prayer recitations for the dead, depending on which family had invited them. And they would all return home from those gatherings with bamboo baskets full of food.

Right at that moment, exactly when the muezzin could be heard blowing into his microphone from the mosque speaker, checking whether his *hello-hello* was sounding yet or not, when the men in their best shirts and sarongs were moving their asses off their front porches to go to the mosque, they saw Mat Dawuk walking down the middle of the village main road.

'*Allahu akbar*! *Allahu akbar*!' the first takbir rang out from the mosque's loudspeaker, followed by another from the mosque's musholla.

Whoever heard those words ringing out should have felt encouraged to repeat them, as they had been taught. But that evening, what they muttered was a prayer for God's forgiveness, their eyes riveted to the spectre in sheer amazement. The men rubbed their chests in concern. The women who caught sight of him stroked their bellies, murmuring prayers for their children, born or as yet unborn. The children who tried to ask what was going on were immediately silenced as their mothers clutched them tightly.

Mat staggered and swayed along the road. Both legs seemed to limp. His swollen left hand clutched his wrecked right shoulder. He was wearing the same shirt and pants he had been wearing when he had been beaten by the mob in front of the health centre seven days ago; they were dishevelled, dirty, encrusted with mud and dried blood. His long, curly hair was like a damp and dirty mat that had been left out in the rain and hung out on the line to dry. In a few places, the hair was clumped and stiff with dried blood stuck to his still festering wounds. In other parts, it was as if the hair was indistinguishable from his skin, with rust coloured cuts and blackening bruises where he had been struck. His face, which always looked terrible, was utterly expressionless.

'*Hayaa alal falaah*! *Hayaa alal falaah*!' The sound of the muezzin called believers to follow the road to grace. But that afternoon, the people of Cottonwood Grove shrunk back, afraid.

Like Javanese people everywhere, the people of Cottonwood Grove believed in wandering ghosts, uneasy spirits and the lost souls of people who had suffered a gruesome or wrongful death. That afternoon, they were sure that was what they were seeing, and so they grew even more certain Mat Dawuk was dead. They were so sure that Mat Dawuk was dead, and this was his roaming spirit, that they looked past the fact that it was too early in the day for anyone's spirit, no matter how lost and no matter how gruesome his death, to be out and about. Even the bravest among the men declined to test their bravery, hasten to the middle of the road, and tackle the wretched, broken body limping along. The women tried with all their might not to scream. A few of them, maybe even with a little compassion or pity, whispered to themselves that the poor, unfortunate soul must be looking for his wife's grave.

The call to prayer came to an end, immediately followed with a song of devotion:

Aja sira banget-banget
Ing mbebeungah ana ing ndunya Malaikat juru pati
Lirak-Lirik marang sira...

This ode to death reminded humankind not to grow too complacent with worldly pleasures and was often heard around the village. The simple, flowing rhyme was easy to remember, so little children often sang it, even when they were absorbed in play. *Do not be so caught up with the things of this world; the Angel of Death has his eye on you.* But, somehow, that afternoon, the song sounded different. With the particular atmosphere of death that had hung over Cottonwood Grove that week, apparently, there was no better afternoon for this verse to be absorbed by its listeners.

The people who would usually cheerfully chat for a moment to one another about this and that before entering the mosque or after exchanging greetings and reciting a few prayers and devotions fell silent. Maybe they all knew that if they opened their mouths, they would be sure to talk about Mat Dawuk's corpse, which had walked along the village road before darkness had fallen. And they remained reserved throughout the *tahlilan* ceremony for the dead, which would usually be coloured with all sorts of conversation. That night there was only the most necessary small talk, about the rats that were threatening the bean harvest, the low price of corn or the rain that hadn't returned after the dramatic downpour of the week before. Even when a few people who lived close to the village graveyard said they had heard the wailing of lamentations from the middle of the cemetery, the others preferred to ignore it.

A slightly different atmosphere took hold when dawn was breaking. The five men on watch were playing Domino on Pak Imam's front veranda, and just as the winning player was slamming down his cards and the loser was swearing at him, they saw a shadow slowly shuffling toward them. As that shadowy figure cohered into a discernible form, it was as if their asses were nailed to the ground. They couldn't stand, let alone run—their mouths hung agape. The figure ascended the stairs to Pak Imam's veranda, passed by them silently, and entered the front door to the house, which had been left open all night, crossing the carpet of woven mats that hadn't been put away since being used for the *tahlilan* the previous day. There was nothing they could do except crane their necks to peer into the front parlour, where that hunched and crooked body stood right before Pak Imam, who had just finished his prayers. That respected man sat dumbfounded in his seat with the Quran open on his lap.

'I did not kill your child,' the figure said, hoarse but clear.

Pak Imam was unable to rise or reply as he realized what was happening and who was speaking to him. The figure turned, walked down the steps of the veranda, and disappeared into the dim light of dawn.

Before the Subuh call to prayer rang out, all of Cottonwood Grove was in an uproar.

Mat Dawuk Must Die Once Again!

Long after that incident, he—Mat Dawuk, I mean—told me himself that he only regained consciousness three days after the death of his wife, was only able to move his body on the fifth day, and struggled with great effort to bend the prison bars in the early morning two days after that. He pretended to faint and then walked out of the police department office, which had been left empty and unattended as the Ashar call to prayer rang out.

It was possible that the police had purposefully vacated their post and were letting him go so they could casually shoot him in the back, saying he had been trying to escape. Someone seeking revenge, a mob or maybe the entire village might have attacked him as soon as they saw him walking down the main road. It's not that he didn't think of these things, but they didn't worry him at all. He should have been dead, so it was nothing for him to face death once more. The most important thing was to know where Inayatun and his child, still in her womb, were buried. So, as long as he was permitted to live, he would know where to make his pilgrimage. And if he had to die, he would know where his soul must go searching.

He knew the Cottonwood Grove village cemetery as well as he knew his own front yard. It was where his mother was buried, the place where, in his derelict and lonely childhood, he had played and even slept. It was the same place where I, for the first time, found a kid of about ten years old, with dishevelled clothes, a filthy body and an ugly face, nodding off next to the gravestone I was seeking. So that was why, even though he arrived there after dark, he had no trouble finding one of the two new graves. He wailed the whole night long, reciting Yasin and Talqin and Tahlil prayers for the dead, lamenting Inayatun and his child, who didn't yet have a name, humming verses from their favourite songs. Just before dawn, he went to his in-laws' house, a house he had never before tried to enter and would have never before been permitted to enter, before returning to the police station to turn himself in.

Now this part, I am willing to bet a finger on it, has never been heard out of anyone in Cottonwood Grove, no matter how honestly they might have told the story because they didn't know about it—maybe they were purposefully kept from knowing. All they knew was, after Ashar on the same day that Mat Dawuk went to Pak Imam's house, there was news from the district that local police forces had just recaptured an escaped prisoner. And that was enough to throw the village in the middle of the forest into another uproar just a few hours after the tumult of that morning.

It could no longer be refuted: this meant Mat Dawuk was still alive. Now it was clear that the figure who had walked along the village road the previous evening and who had met with Pak Imam at his house early in the morning had not been his ghost, but Mat Dawuk himself. Mat Dawuk was still breathing, even though his bones were fractured and his body was battered and bruised. Now they were regretting, really and truly regretting, that they had let the police come, had even helped them drag his limp and blood-stained body and throw it into the patrol car without first making sure that the son-of-a-bitch was dead. Whether they liked it or not, now the people of Cottonwood Grove had to admit that, just as they had heard it being said, that Satan-faced bastard who they had looked down upon ever since he was a child indeed had nine lives.

Now, the only path left for them to finish him was to take him to court.

'I will offer everything I have, my fields and my rice paddies, everything I own, to have that man publicly hanged—and chopped into pieces, too, if possible!' Pak Imam fumed in front of the crowd attending the memorial, held forty days after Inayatun's death.

'However much the prosecutor asks, whatever the judge wants, I'll give it to them, as long as that son-of-a-bitch is sentenced to death. Wawasan 2020 and an independent Malaysia is still a long way off. UMNO is still in control of Parliament. Ringgits are still scattered across the streets of Malaysia; all that's left is to scoop them up,' boasted Hanan, Foreman Har's brother-in-law, who was also Woodsman Hasan's older brother. Hanan had been a degenerate and a hopelessly incapable youth, and his father hadn't trusted him enough to bequeath him the family sawmill. But his luck changed completely after marrying Haryati, Ranger Hartoyo's daughter, and going abroad to Malaysia. Now, he was known to be the richest migrant, with the best house, in all of Cottonwood Grove.

No less ferocious than his older brother was Woodsman Hasan. Still fervently repeating how Mat Dawuk had slaughtered two people who loved each other—which is how he was now describing Inayatun and Foreman Har—he vowed to do whatever it took to get justice for his dear friend.

'Right now, if there is anyone who will put an offer on my sawmill and all of its equipment, its hundreds of planks, and its paper, I will sell it, and I will use all the money to pay anyone who can guarantee to finish that cursed devil once and for all. What value does material wealth hold when compared to true friendship? If necessary, I will sell my soul!' he declared, drawing his finger across his throat. Of course, while saying all that, he was careful to watch his mouth so that he didn't let slip how he had scuttled away after splitting his friend's chest open with his hatchet.

So as not to appear silent at the unfortunate death of one of his ranks, a forest police representative who had come to attend the forty-day memorial for Foreman Har also staunchly declared that his agency would rally all their energy and effort to ensure that Foreman Har's killer would be prosecuted to the fullest extent of the law. He also promised that Foreman Har would receive a posthumous raise in rank since he had died in the course of duty. But at the 100-day memorial, the man returned with a weaker statement—that low-level officer had been warned by his superiors not to speak out of turn. Aside from the issue of whoever had killed Foreman Har, the police findings reported that the killing was motivated by an act of infidelity, and that did not reflect favourably on their organization. 'We will be following the legal case as it unfolds,' was all he said.

All kinds of talk—from those full of rage, those pretending to be full of rage, and those just following along—and it seemed that no one in Cottonwood Grove disagreed with the will of Inayatun's and Foreman Har's families. It could be no other way: Mat Dawuk had to die.

Once again.

Dulawi's Reappearance

PAK IMAM AND Hanan didn't need to spend that much to ensure Mat Dawuk was thrown into prison. The judge and prosecutor didn't have to be forced into their decision—if they had been forced, they certainly would have pronounced a completely different verdict. From start to finish, it could be considered a straightforward murder case, mainly because of how Mat Dawuk handled it.

Don't think Mat Dawuk would weep, like Rhoma Irama wailing in the film *Begadang* when he was found guilty of killing a woman and being put in chains: 'The innocent is locked away, the guilty laugh and do not pay!' Mat Dawuk wasn't like that. Even though he had privately told his father-in-law, who refused to acknowledge him, that he didn't kill his wife, in court, Mat stoically accepted the prosecutor's charges that he had murdered Inayatun and Foreman Har.

Had Mat Dawuk surrendered? Anyone who suggested such a thing would of course have been totally wrong. There was no expression of defeat on his ugly face, which, even after healing from his wounds, looked more damaged than ever, nor would it be accurate to say that he had submitted to God's will. Observant folks would see that what appeared on Mat's face was an expression of despondent apathy. Simple thinkers might have just called him crazy—yes, after killing his wife he had gone crazy.

Mat Dawuk was sentenced to twelve years in jail. That decision didn't satisfy many, but what more did they want? Right at the moment when he was most needed, Woodsman Hasan, who had been valiant and brave with a mouth stinking of palm wine, disappeared. Forget sacrificing all of his belongings and his very soul to avenge his friend—he didn't even show up in court to offer a few words of testimony! It was said he feared coming face-to-face with Mat Dawuk, terrified the court would actually turn against him. And so, despite being a key witness, he decided to sneak away from Cottonwood Grove—people later discovered his older brother had helped him get to Malaysia. Those who were asked to take his place, testified perfunctorily—it was lucky that they weren't accused of perjury.

But to those with good memories, Mat Dawuk's trial wasn't memorable because of the disappearance of a key witness or because of an all too easy acceptance of the prosecutor's charges by the accused, even though the case unfolded in his favour. And it wasn't because he received a sentence too light for someone who had confessed to killing two people. Instead, the surprise witness was the star. He appeared unpredictably and out of nowhere, like the Pak Haji character in those *Suzanna* films, to testify on behalf of the accused, and he gave a testimony so convincing it should have freed Mat Dawuk—if the justice system had been working correctly. His account made so much sense that the judge could barely believe it. Even so, Mat was sentenced to twelve years because he had accepted the charges against him.

Mat Dawuk was practically tried without a lawyer. I say practically because although he couldn't pay a cent, he was represented by a shoddy state-appointed attorney. When it was time to call witnesses to the stand in his defence, Mat didn't know who he was supposed to call. Inayatun had been the only person in his life, and this trial was being held to convict him for murdering her. He did have one other relative, who he called his uncle, but was reluctant to ask the man to come forward—Mat was loath to call on anyone to testify on his behalf, and figured the guy didn't know anything anyway.

But right at that moment Mbah Dulawi, his grandfather, astonishingly and inexplicably appeared.

Have you ever studied the figure of the guru in old Hong Kong kung-fu films? If you look closely, you will see someone still young, with a robust body and tight skin, under the wig of white hair, stuck-on white moustache and a long white fake beard. That was how Mbah Dulawi looked when he appeared on the witness stand—the only difference was that his hair, moustache and beard were real.

His hair was long, wavy and white with a gilding of golden yellow from decades of smoking tobacco. That same yellow could be found in his beard and his white undershirt. There was a flat black *kopiah* cap made in Bungah, Gresik, on his head. It had once been black, but the bottom rim had faded to sepia from years of ablutions. His faded batik shirt was paired with a frayed Maduran sarong.

Cottonwood Grove and Deep Well villagers with good memories would recognize these clothes he wore in court as those he most often wore to Friday prayers, and they would also see that, while his hair was whiter and longer, his face hadn't changed at all since he had disappeared into the forest twenty-three years ago. He moved slowly towards the witness stand but he walked without a cane. With every step, the wooden clog sandals that he was wearing—the same ones he used to wear to the mosque—let out a clack, and the rhythm resounded through the courtroom that had been silenced by his appearance.

'I am Abdullah Alawi,' he stated. 'Muhammad Dawud's grandfather.' When the judge looked doubtful, he took a tobacco pouch from the folds of his sarong and pulled out his identity card from 1971. He also held out his Masyumi Party membership card, which was even older—from before the party was banned, of course, and written in the old-fashioned spelling so that the name of the party read 'Masjoemi'.

Without having to be asked much else, he told what he knew about the bloody events of the afternoon in question. He started with when Mat left Inayatun for the forest after their small argument and met Foreman Har and Woodsman Hasan at the acacia tree; then recounted the conversation the three men had, which wasn't about anything significant but determined what would happen next; how Mat had picked corn and beans and set out to find the *kecacil* fruit for his wife, encountered an ill omen and hurried home; and how arriving at his house, he found his wife already drenched with blood. On the other hand, he also testified that after meeting Mat Dawuk, Foreman Har and Woodsman Hasan sped their dirt bikes towards the village, both drunk; the motorbike Foreman Har was driving turned towards Mat Dawuk's cow shed, where Inayatun was alone. They parked their dirt bikes in the yard, and both knocked on the door. Inayatun reluctantly opened the door and warily invited them in. Foreman Har and Woodsman Hasan entered politely as guests, but it didn't take long to realize that they had other intentions. Foreman Har started the conversation by asking about the same things he had asked about when he had come to the house three days earlier: about the forest land that Mat was working, how it was growing and if there were any problems, whether they had been given enough seeds and whether these had been planted yet, and reminded Inayatun to address the matter of her father's cow shed being on state-owned forest land. Inayatun responded as necessary and tried to communicate her discomfort, but her two guests didn't seem to care, and Foreman Har even pretended to inquire after Mat Dawuk, asking where he was. Inayatun lied and said that Mat Dawuk was drawing water from the spring and would be back any minute, but of course Foreman Har and Woodsman Hasan knew that wasn't true. Inayatun politely hinted that she'd like them to leave by saying that she was in the middle of cooking and couldn't entertain them. Inayatun turned to go, trying to make her two guests uncomfortable, but instead, Foreman Har followed her and grabbed her waist from behind. Inayatun struggled, asking to be let go and threatening Foreman Har that Mat would be there any minute. Foreman Har, who knew Mat Dawuk would not be there any time soon, instead tightened his embrace; because her threats were ineffective, Inayatun said that she would scream that he was trying to rape her; Foreman Har burst out laughing. Woodsman Hasan joined in and reminded Inayatun that even if anyone heard her scream, everyone in Cottonwood Grove knew she was the easiest woman in the village. Inayatun kept struggling, and Foreman Har became bolder in his liberties. Inayatun tried to escape him; 'I'm pregnant,' she pleaded.

'Wow, what luck,' Foreman Har replied with a grin, 'If I have any influence, your child will have a more passable face.'

Foreman Har began to slide his hands all over Inayatun's waist and then raised them to her breasts while Woodsman Hasan swiftly locked the front door from the inside. Not knowing any other way to free herself, Inayatun fought with all her might. Foreman Har, who hadn't expected such fierce resistance, was surprised, released his hold and Inayatun ran to the kitchen. Foreman Har quickly cornered Inayatun, but now she was holding a kitchen knife. Foreman Har and Woodsman Hasan tried to convince Inayatun to be more agreeable, but Inayatun was already wild with fear. She stabbed her knife in every direction, screaming threats; because Foreman Har and Woodsman Hasan did not retreat, Inayatun began to lunge at them with the knife; then, a scuffle ensued.

At first, it was between Foreman Har and Inayatun, but Woodsman Hasan joined in when he saw Foreman Har was overwhelmed. Finally, Woodsman Hasan was able to cover Inayatun's mouth, and Foreman Har grabbed her knife, but right as he grabbed it he realized that it was already dripping with blood; the knife had accidentally stabbed Inayatun's stomach. Foreman Har recoiled from Inayatun's bloody body, shaking to see the knife in his hand, which now was also covered in blood, while close by, Woodsman Hasan stood with his face aghast; at that moment, the door was broken down from outside, and Mat Dawuk came bursting into the house, finding Inayatun lying twitching on the floor with her stomach torn open, Foreman Har still holding the knife, and Woodsman Hasan acting as though he had no idea what was going on.

Angrily, Mat Dawuk lunged towards Foreman Har; panicked, Foreman Har flung the knife and felt for the pistol at his hip. Mat Dawuk had no trouble immobilizing Foreman Har, who was terrified. Mat Dawuk's left hand closed around Foreman Har's throat while his right hand twisted Foreman Har's right arm and pointed the pistol right between the owner's ribs; all Mat Dawuk had left to do was burrow his fingers into the skin of Foreman Har's neck and yank on his windpipe or push the muzzle of the forest police issued pistol into the chest of its owner and pull the trigger. Still, Mat Dawuk stopped and turned to see the body of his wife, sprawled out, her life draining away. That was when, from behind Mat Dawuk's back, Woodsman Hasan lunged forward, swinging his hatchet. Mat Dawuk dodged just one step to the side while releasing the grip of his left hand on Foreman Har's neck. Suddenly, Woodsman Hasan's hatchet, which had been aimed with all his might at Mat Dawuk's back, instead plunged squarely into Foreman Har's chest up to the hilt, tearing his green uniform and splitting his breastbone. Blood gushed from Foreman Har's gaping wound, wetting his green shirt, spraying across Mat Dawuk's face and the farming clothes he was wearing; Foreman Har slumped down, legs bent and head lolling. Mat Dawuk hurried to his wife, picked her up and ran, carrying her along the village road, heading for the Galeng Gede Community Health Centre, ignoring Woodsman Hasan, who was stumbling through the untended gardens toward the village in a wild panic, screaming that Mat Dawuk had just killed Inayatun and Foreman Har.

'That's what happened, Your Honor,' Mbah Dulawi concluded his testimony.

Everyone in the courtroom was thunderstruck: It was complete, convincing and made perfect sense. Forget Woodsman Hasan, that coward; if Foreman Har could be risen from the dead to refute that testimony, he would certainly be at a loss to come up with a different story. If there was any doubt about the testimony, it was that the story was *too* complete, *too* perfect. How could someone know about the meeting between Foreman Har, Woodsman Hasan, and Mat Dawuk at the acacia tree, know exactly what Mat Dawuk had done in his fields, and at the same time follow the journey of the motorbike that Foreman Har drove straight to Inayatun's house? And think, if he hadn't been at the cow shed, then how could he depict each event, leading up to and including the murders, so clearly and completely?

To the small group of Mat Modar's former students who knew Dulawi, also known as Abdullah Dulawi, well, there was nothing incredible about it, but the story was difficult for the judge to accept, even though it had far fewer holes than the sequence of events provided by the police and the prosecutors. On top of that, Mat Dawuk had not explicitly denied the accusations against him. Ultimately, the only effect of Mbah Dulawi's testimony was to make the judge reluctant to impose the maximum sentence requested by the prosecutor, which was the death penalty.

This, of course, was still a big blow to those who wished the saga of Mat Dawuk would come to a swift end. Forced to be satisfied with a sentence of twelve years in prison for a confessed killer, Inayatun's and Foreman Har's families and the people of Cottonwood Grove had to find some other way to obliterate Mat Dawuk.

Even so, it was not just the light sentence that made their gorges rise and the blood pool in their skulls. It was, in fact, Mbah Dulawi's sudden appearance that made them shake, their hands clutching at their chests. You all must know: this is not just about the reappearance of a man who had been thought dead for more than twenty-three years. This is about the boiling over of a simmering rage, a grudge that had been nursed for three generations.

The Three Generation Grudge

You all are asking what Mbah Dulawi did after his sudden reappearance. You may as well ask what happens to the coffee I drink after it goes down my throat. Now, I think I can tell the difference between shit that is black from a cup of coffee and shit that is black from a bleeding ulcer, but can I guarantee?

I don't know, just like nobody else knows. He disappeared as soon as he stepped off the witness stand, just like that, in the same mysterious way he had appeared. No one in the state courthouse, including me, could see him any longer. Poof, he appeared! Poof, he was gone! So, yeah, *wallahu alam*...That's why some claimed he hadn't even given the testimony in court, and the story wasn't true. But those who had seen him with their eyes, sitting there on the stand as plain as day, would insist it must have been his ghost.

Nevertheless, I will tell you what he did before disappearing twenty-three years earlier and why he played such an important part in the multi-generational chain of enmity between the forest police and the poor woodcutters.

Or, as they called it, between the System and the Villains. For that, we must go back a few more decades. What you are listening to is a story of revenge that is almost as old as a free and independent Indonesia. Do you understand? But before I do that, I need a new hot coffee. Agreed?

Great!

First, just one question: Are you all familiar with Mat Modar? Or maybe you've heard his name.

Ah, just as I expected. Just as I expected! And if I may make a guess, you heard it from me, right? And you probably didn't believe what I was saying.

Allah Karim…

Folks, order yourself another because starting now, you'd better drink plenty of coffee. Then, if the Angel of Death should come for you, you won't be empty—even if you are short on brains, at least you'll be full of something other than full of shit!

Now, listen up.

Mat Modar, that's what people called him. His real name was Ahmad Mudzar, but because of his actions and the stories that surrounded him, people preferred to call him Mat Modar—Mat Modar, who always cheats death; that's what people called him if they wanted to be more specific. He was notorious but also secretive and had been involved in all kinds of escapades, from the time of forced planting under the Dutch until Indonesia won its independence. If you are willing to believe it, there were even those who said he had been a member of the Sentot Prawirodirjo troops, which dispersed after being captured by Prince Dipenegoro at the end of the Javanese War.

During those times, there was no one in the forest towns on the eastern part of Java's northern coast who didn't know his name or what he did. People knew who his enemies were and made sure to be considered among his friends, but at the same time, there was no one who could say for sure how old he was, where he came from or where he had been born.

He was probably a little bit older than the founders of the country, Bung Karno and Bung Hatta. That would have made sense, but the strange thing was, people had plenty of stories about how he had joined the revolt of the warriors and *kyai* against the Government back when the Javanese were forced to plant only sugarcane and tobacco, whenever that was, exactly—my brother here certainly must know. So, they say, he knew several figures that we have only heard of in stories and *ludruk* shows: Joko Sambang from Gangsir Mountain, Bambang Sutejo from Bromo Valley, Sarip Tambak Oso from Surabaya, even Raden Branjang Kawat from Madura. At the same time, there was another stockpile of stories that associated him with the people's fight against Japan.

These days, he could easily be called a warrior or even a hero. But when he was alive, it wasn't so simple. Colonial officials and Dutch security forces considered him a bad guy. Greedy landowners thought he was an upstart, vicious native overseers thought he was a troublemaker, and the rich but stingy haji considered him a robber, a thief, a menace. No forest service officers, from Rembang to Madiun, could keep their cool during a run-in with him.

He was a friend to the marginalized, the forgotten,

the cast aside. He would stop by unannounced at the house of old widows, bringing sacks of rice and fish that he had gotten from somewhere. He would sometimes appear among the exhausted woodcutters who were being persecuted by the forest rangers, bringing them fresh water or a jug of palm wine. He voluntarily served as the clever mouth and nimble fists of poor folks trapped in debt to moneylenders.

People talked a lot about his unassuming figure. He was short and slight and limped due to a crooked leg. Wherever he went, he wore shabby clothes with a sarong wrapped around his neck. He didn't wear long loose pants like most warriors, but a pair of dark green shorts, a gift from the founder of a scout training in Surabaya, who he greatly respected. It was said that wherever he went, he carried a *keket*, a small sickle with a blunt tip that women usually used to weed or trim grass. With all this, he cut quite a different figure than an elite warrior or a magic whiz—he looked more like a farmer heading for the gardens out behind his house. Yet with that sickle, he and his fellow fighters turned the cane fields and sugar factories in Tapal Kuda topsy-turvy and struck fear into the hearts of the Dutch security forces, who were so cruel during the Great Depression. And, believe it or not, it was also with that sickle that he would occasionally join the woodcutters in the forest to chop down teak. One story tells of how he was sent to Digoel, but another version, where he was exiled to Sawahlunto in Sumatera, makes much more sense—although there is the possibility that both of these are true, who can be sure? With the guerrilla fighters and, of course, with that small sickle in his hand, he beat back the Japanese troops at the mouth of the Solo River. Mat Modar was invincible until finally, one of his students, his favourite student, sold his secret to the Kenpeitai Military Police. And it was on the blade of a Japanese soldier's bayonet, so they say, that Mat Modar met his end.

Mat Modar's origins were unclear—he wasn't known to have any family, he never stayed in one place very long, and no one is sure where he was buried. Even so, at the very least, he had two students. The older and smarter one was named Nurkalil, and the younger one was named Dulawi. Nurkalil was bright and full of aspirations—what people today would call ambitious maybe because he was the son of an affluent fish farm owner on the Gresik coast. Unlike Dulawi, the son of a poor peasant in Cottonwood Grove, a simple and quict man, even though he would ultimately become better known for his bravery. These different backgrounds and characters made these two take such different paths.

Nurkalil, it is said, traded the secret of his guru's weakness for rank and a position in the Tegal-Pekalongan local government. And that's why people who dislike him call him Nur *Kalir*, which more or less means Nur, who is always hungry, who's greedy, who's never satisfied—what in Javanese we call *nggragas*. When the people rioted against the regional officials there, not long after Indonesia won independence, Nurkalil was on the wrong side. And that was when he met his end. Sakyani, a local brawler who knew Mat Modar well, beat Nurkalil in a fight.

Dulawi, whose brilliance wasn't necessarily evident,

followed his guru everywhere, especially in his last moments—or at least, he was there the last time Mat Modar was seen alive, being drawn and tortured by the Japanese. He had wanted to help, but his guru had forbidden him to intervene. Once Mat Modar was believed dead at the hands of the Japanese, Dulawi joined the guerrillas, going in and out of the forest as long as the resistance lasted, first fighting against the remaining Japanese soldiers and then facing the Allies. But he still wasn't that well-known, sometimes even underestimated, except by his friends in the struggle, the enemies he faced, and ultimately, the forest service.

After the war, Dulawi married a young woman from Deep Well Village, the neighbouring village to Cottonwood Grove. The old commander of his troop made him an offer to formally join the army, but he refused. He chose to move into his wife's house and live simply. He was skilled at treating and weaving bamboo and making walls, baskets, and kitchen supplies. His hands were nimble with a *caluk*, the curved double blade with all kinds of uses but especially suited for splitting and whittling bamboo. And maybe that's why some people called him Dul Caluk. He built a humble prayer house and there he taught the village children what he knew: prayer recitation and self-defence. But that small, simple prayer house eventually led to a big, complicated problem.

This is the story. Dulawi built the prayer house with his own hands, more or less in secret. He scraped together the beams and floorboards from planks he had saved during the war, filling in the gaps with scraps from small woodcutting jobs, and he planned to make the walls out of woven bamboo. But of course, such a secret wouldn't last long. Building a prayer house at that time was not easy and was usually a collective effort. His neighbours and others who respected him found out about the project and pressed their help upon him. Dulawi couldn't refuse.

One day, a woodcutter came to Dulawi's house, black and blue, his back full of welts from being whipped and his face battered and bruised. The man said three foremen had intercepted him while he was chopping down wood the night before. They took his axe and dragged him to the forestry headquarters.

There, Overseer Harjo beat him with the branch of a young teak tree. He asked what he was 'stealing' the teak for and he was forced to reply that the wood would be donated to Dulawi's prayer house. 'You tell Dulawi,' Overseer Harjo said, according to the unfortunate woodsman, 'that if he wants to make a prayer house from teak, he must plant the seeds, rather than helping himself to government wood!'

Dulawi didn't say anything then, other than to comfort the poor woodsman and tend to his wounds with some spit and some spells. But that night, he told his wife he was going out into the forest. He didn't forget to bring his faithful *caluk*. He knew the woods quite well and knew exactly where he needed to go. He chose the biggest and best teak trunk. With his *caluk*, he hacked that trunk down himself, and before dawn, it was a large log ready to be hauled. But because it had not been girdled and the bark had not been stripped, the log was quite heavy. Usually, it would take at least four strapping woodsmen to lift it, but Dulawi easily shouldered it himself. He didn't bring the log home but carried it straight to Overseer Harjo's home in Cottonwood Grove.

Dulawi knocked on the door politely. '*Assalamu alaikum*, Mr Overseer.' Subuh had just passed.

Because it was so early in the morning, Overseer Harjo opened the door grumpily and only grew angrier when he saw Dulawi standing before him with a teak log at his feet and the *caluk* in his hand.

'What do you want?' he snapped.

'Teak has made you rich and powerful, but unlike us, the woodcutters, you've never worked to plant or chop it down. Maybe, from time to time, it might do you some good to hold it in your own two hands.'

Overseer Harjo immediately understood this had to do with the woodsman he had punished, but he still couldn't guess what Dulawi wanted exactly.

'Please, go ahead, sir,' Dulawi repeated his request. He spoke in polite Javanese, like any woodsman speaking to a member of the forest service, but as he spoke, Dulawi raised the *caluk* in his hand to his shoulder, like a woodsman shouldering an axe.

Anyone who had heard the stories about Dulawi and his *caluk* would have been afraid—and so was Overseer Harjo.

'Ah, you're joking around so early in the morning, Dul,' he said. The tone of his voice had changed. 'Come in, let's have some coffee,' he continued with a false invitation.

'Go ahead, please, pick it up, sir,' Dulawi repeated, and

this time it sounded more like an order. He thrust his chin towards the tree trunk and tightened his grip on the *caluk* handle. Overseer Harjo's bloated body began to tremble.

'Well, of course, there's no way I'm strong enough, Dul,' he said, laughing the laugh of a frightened man.

'I'm just a lowly woodsman, and I'm strong enough, sir. Surely you, an Overseer, must be strong enough, too. Just try it, sir,' Dulawi pressed.

Reluctant and afraid, Overseer Harjo bent down and wrapped his two thick but flabby arms around the teak log. His arms were a bit shorter than those of the average man in Cottonwood Grove, so he could only reach about halfway around, and when he tried to lift it, the log didn't budge.

'Try a bit harder, sir!' Now, Dulawi was clearly ordering him. And, with no other choice, Overseer Harjo did what Dulawi asked. But, just as he knew it would be, his effort was fruitless. Gasping for breath, his back in shooting pain, he stepped back and gave up.

'I'm really not strong enough, Dul.'

'If you can't do it alone, then let me help you.'

Dulawi bent down, wrapped his arms around the log lying on the ground, and lifted it easily. Overseer Harjo stood there stunned when Dulawi placed the heavy log on his right shoulder like a father teaching his son how to carry a bundle of grass for the first time. Overseer Harjo was trapped under the log. A loud crack, like the snapping of bone, was followed by a howl of agony.

At that howl, all the neighbours came running out of their houses, but as soon as they saw who was there, they stopped short. As they all looked on, Dulawi calmly walked away, the *caluk* on his shoulder and the large teak log he had chopped down the night before lying there on the ground with Overseer Harjo's rotund body squashed beneath it.

Overseer Harjo's family and the forestry service tried to indict Dulawi, but no one dared give witness and so the case never went to court. Overseer Harjo was spared from death, but his suffering had just begun. His long life was spent lying on a day bed—his spine had been crushed, and it never healed. For decades, Overseer Harjo lived, full of rage at his paralysis, while his grandchildren had to clean his piss and shit, wipe his drool, and listen to his never-ending stream of profanity.

When they looked at Dulawi, they longed for revenge; it could not be otherwise. Not knowing how else to satisfy their grudge, they first went the cowardly and improper route, trying to get him with black magic. But they chose the wrong target. Dulawi was not Mat Modar's most impressive student. He would be the first to say he was nothing compared to his guru, even compared to his fellow students. But he was still Dulawi, also known as Dul Caluk.

Of course, after a while, they did find a way to vent some of their ill will through that wayward son—again, I beg you, don't force me to say his name.

The whole uproar of Gestok—isn't that what Sukarno called the attempted coup in '65?—and everything that came after wasn't too crazy in this area, not like it was to the west and the south. But that doesn't mean that no one here was affected. Two members of Uden Ireng in Cucukan were taken, and only one returned. An elementary school teacher in Deep Well Village, who was a member of the leftist Non-Vaksentral teacher's union, was also called in. He returned safely, but he could never teach again.

The rest mainly were those involved with the People's Youth. I didn't hear that any of them were executed, but quite a few were thrown in jail, and for years after their release, they were kept under surveillance and forced to regularly report to the local authorities. Of course, they weren't members of the People's Youth, let alone communists; a few of them used to pray with me, a few were just big-mouthed kids who wanted to redistribute the land of this or that rich haji and some others were attending rehearsals for *misri* or *ludruk* theatre performances, and the rest just liked to dash around and jostle each other while playing soccer—and it was one from this last bunch that got Dulawi into so much trouble.

One morning, after a night in the forest, Dulawi came home to find his wife in tears. She said that their son—that wayward kid, who at that time was still a teenager—had been taken by soldiers. They said he was a member of the People's Youth and accused him of planning an opposition attack in retaliation for the crackdown on the Communist Party. They even claimed they had confiscated a firearm as proof. Dulawi knew his son was innocent—either they had mistaken him for someone else, or more likely, someone had accused his son to destroy him. And if that was the case, he knew who was responsible.

Dulawi also knew where to look. Luckily, even though

his face had been kicked by soldiers' boots all night long, the kid had not yet been taken anywhere far away.

Knowing the military resort commander well, Dulawi said the boy was his son and the firearm in question was a guerrilla artefact. Then he took out his Masyumi card to show the soldiers—the same card that he took out years later in the court that was trying his grandson—and the child, not knowing how lucky he was, was brought home in one piece.

'Stop playing soccer,' Dulawi reprimanded his son. 'And stop spending time with Overseer Harjo's son.' Dulawi suspected that Overseer Harjo's son, later known as Ranger Hartoyo, was behind his son's arrest—and this was the case.

But his son was stubborn. He was a foolish kid. He wasn't just bad at picking friends; he couldn't even recognize his father's enemies. He didn't play soccer anymore because no one played it anymore since most of the players—who weren't as lucky as him—now spent all their time reporting to the military resort command. As the months went by, and he spent more time hanging out with Hartoyo, he began to enjoy cockfighting, and his dirty mouth began to enjoy palm wine.

Dulawi had been able to get his son's body home safely, but he could never bring his heart back home. As time passed, the relationship between father and son grew ever more distant, and in the end, could not be salvaged. The child grew more errant and disobedient. When he developed a taste for alcohol, Dulawi held his tongue—Dulawi didn't drink, he didn't like to, but Mat Modar, his guru, indulged from time to time—but when his son began to enjoy prostitution, Dulawi tried to beat some sense into him.

The problem was that the beating didn't at all deter his wayward son—instead, their relationship grew worse. And this had dire consequences for Dulawi's wife, a simple woman who adored her child. Dulawi's wife was distraught, her heart succumbed to a despair that ruined her health and ultimately killed her. Feeling responsible for her death, Dulawi was devastated.

He tried to atone by marrying his depraved son to the girl he wanted, hoping that through this marriage, their relationship might improve and, more importantly, his son might change his ways. But instead, everything deteriorated. Without a doubt, this was the worst decision Dulawi ever made because, you all know that to soothe his son's heart and fulfil his wishes, Dulawi had to deny the wishes and break the heart of another son, a child he loved as well as his own, even though he wasn't a child by blood, someone who, because he isn't very important to this story, I don't need to name. But after all that, it turned out the decision was no help at all and resulted in nothing but more grief.

True, there were signs of change after Dulawi married his errant son to the girl he desired. He stopped gallivanting, drank less, and stopped going to whorehouses. But, after Mat Dawuk's mother died giving birth to him, he despised that ugly child. He blamed his son for his wife's death and his misfortune, and in the end, he also blamed his father for ruining his life. Their relationship grew worse.

There was nothing else Dulawi could do to intervene, but at the same time, he could not bear his feeling of loss as a parent. After a painful fight with his worthless child, as everyone can attest, Dulawi went into the forest and never appeared again—that is, until he showed himself in Mat Dawuk's trial, twenty-three years later.

Witnessing Dulawi undone by his son must have been pleasing for Overseer Harjo's descendants. But it didn't seem commensurate with their father's ruin, which led to the decline of their family's prestige in the forestry service ever after. And when they saw Dulawi appear in court, looking hale and hearty, and what's more, trying to defend Mat Dawuk against the charges of killing Foreman Har, they realized that the score still wasn't settled. There was still business to take care of. Their grudge was still alive and well. Their revenge was not complete.

But how could that revenge be taken? Even when the head of their family had been an Overseer, they hadn't been able to put Dulawi in prison. Now they only had a Foreman—and he was dead. And who was even left to be the target of this revenge? Dulawi had disappeared again in the same bizarre way that he had reappeared.

The only one they could get to now was Mat Dawuk. But the recent events had made it plain: this hideous grandson was just as tough as his grandfather.

The Demon Butcher Busts Out of His Grave and Seeks Revenge

And my mouth will also toughen if it doesn't fill with smoke soon. Where are the cigarettes? Come on, give me two! This story still has a long way to go.

Great!

Now, my mouth will be soft and supple; my tongue has loosened up once again. And so, let's get back to Mat Dawuk.

Tough guy Mat Dawuk did not serve even two-thirds of his sentence. He was released from prison not long after participating in his seventh Independence Day assembly in jail, for…what do they call it? Ah, yes: remission.

'They didn't grant me my freedom. They just didn't want the trouble of dealing with me,' that's what he told me once he was out—if you believe me, great, if you don't, you don't!

Even though he hadn't gotten the death penalty, Mat Dawuk knew he would not be left in peace. He claimed that he had fended off all sorts of witchcraft, all kinds of black magic, while he was in jail. When that didn't work, they were at no loss to think up ways to harass him. One time, three men were thrown into his cell, supposedly for a case of stolen wood, but it didn't take long for him to realize that they were really after him and were hired to kill him. Unfortunately, whoever paid them didn't know what they could do and, of course, didn't know what their target was capable of. The men were just low-class thugs, that's what Mat Dawuk said, and because it would be ridiculous to die at the hands of hired toughs with such middling ability, Mat Dawuk took them out.

'Maybe the prison warden didn't want the headache, and the guards were tired of beating me up, they let me go for some made-up good behaviour, maybe so they wouldn't have to worry about getting pulled into the fray if something happened to me or happened because of me,' he sneered.

With his cleft lip and face broken beyond repair, he looked hideous. His face never lit up again, even after he was free. He didn't know what his freedom was for. He no longer desired the world outside the prison walls; he no longer had any business with any of it. He had no plans for the rest of his life, even though he was the age of a young father with a seven-year-old kid. Ah, when he talked about his unborn child, who died along with his wife, he would choke up a bit, but he never broke down and cried, and good thing—if he was ugly when he smiled, imagine how he would have looked if he had wept.

'So, what is my life for?' he asked with a self-mocking grin. If that question was being put to me, I would have had no answer.

'You're not looking for revenge?' I asked in return, to provoke him. At that time, Woodsman Hasan was still alive, and word was he was living in Malaysia.

Once again, he just smiled. He got my meaning. He admitted, at the beginning, that his rage at Woodsman Hasan had given him the motivation to stay alive. Maybe the only reason he had survived the mob attack in front of the community health centre was because he had seen Woodsman Hasan's face in the crowd. Then, in prison, remembering his face—his terrified face a moment after he had impaled his friend, his self-righteous face when he was on the front lines of the attack—made Mat Dawuk itch to bend the prison bars, hunt him down wherever he ran, crack his head open with his own hatchet, and hack him into tiny pieces until no one would be able to tell the difference between Woodsman Hasan's head and that of a sacrificial goat. But, at the same time, his promise to Inayatun that he would never kill again nagged at him. That was the only thing holding him back.

'What about against the people of Cottonwood Grove?' I pressed him.

He shook his head, then smiled again. 'I'm tired,' he said. He explained that it was his grudge and resentment against the people of Cottonwood Grove that had turned him into a hot-blooded youth and then shaped him into a cold-blooded killer. And, no doubt about it, he had suffered. But worst of all, he had made the people he loved suffer.

Again and again, he said, almost as if he was trying to convince himself, that maybe Inayatun's death was his karma. He had killed people. Of course, most of them had been scum: predatory men who ruined women, foul traffickers who sold people cheap, deceitful foremen who reneged on their employees' wages. He didn't need to mourn people like that. But maybe one or two of them weren't as crooked as he had thought.

Remorse like that was enough to convince him that he had caused Inayatun's death—especially when he remembered how stubbornly he had ignored the cues that his wife had given him. 'Ah, forget carrying her from our house to the fields. If I had known what was going to happen, I would have carried her for the rest of my life, as long as I could protect her.'

'It wasn't you who killed your wife,' I reminded him.

'But it's because of me she was killed,' he replied.

If he felt guilty, there was little I could say to change his mind. So all I could do was ask, 'So, what are your plans?'

He shook his head. 'I don't know.'

It was heavy. I could understand his anxiety and the loss of his spirit. I understood how hollow it felt to have no purpose in life while death also declined to come for you—and don't think this is just me quoting the lyrics to a *dangdut* song!

People must live for something, whether it's happiness, riches, rank, degree, pleasure, a dream, or whatever. Even the Demon Butcher, Wiro Sableng's evil enemy, struggled tooth and nail to bust out of his grave, dragging himself along with his two arms, scraping his shins, because he was seeking revenge!

Since Inayatun's death, Mat Dawuk had nothing to defend or fight for.

'Go see your grandfather,' I suggested.

'Would Mbah Dul want to see me?'

'I don't know. But I think you need to talk to him.'

After that, he disappeared. I don't know whether he saw his grandfather or not.

But a little while later, I heard that he had been spotted back in Malaysia.

Everything Changes—Everything But This

After almost sixteen years, five presidents have come and gone. A lot has changed in this country and in Cottonwood Grove, too.

Just like all the villages on the eastern part of the northern coast of Java touched by Malaysian money, at night, even towns on the edge of the forest that were the last to get electricity shine much brighter. Seen from the heavens, they are like large globed lamps around a giant, lush park. There are no more traditional *limas* houses with teak posts at all four corners, walls from plaited bamboo, and the inside divided into two simple rooms. You catch a chill in houses like that, the old folks said. They're old-fashioned, said the younger ones. The neighbours will talk, the wives said.

So, the best sand from Bojonegoro was sent for, the most expensive cement from Gresik, the most excellent red brick from Mojokerto, the strongest gypsum from Sidoarjo, the thickest tile from Kebumen, and the most skilled stone masonry from Lerok—by the men they say built the Petronas Twin Towers. The result was grand houses taller than teak trees, wider than the forest they worked, with many rooms arranged in floor-plans as intricate as the spiralling tendrils of a bitter yam, with walls painted in bright 'made in Japan' colours, and slanted sills. The front yards used to have rose apple, mango, or coconut trees, complete with a tethered goat, a chicken coop or a stone trough where the oxen could drink. But that was before. Now, front yards have become parks, with flowers blooming in pots lined up in neat rows, lampposts, wooden statues made in Ngawi, and, of course, a garage, exactly like the houses of officials in Putrajaya in Malaysia. If you all went into these houses hoping to find a stack of corn tied with its husks or half-dried cassava spread out on top of a tarp, its fragrance filling the whole space, well, you came at the wrong time. That was in the past. Those days are gone, boss. Instead, you'll find furniture with arms and backrests carved in the Jepara style—even though they're knockoffs—with cushions as soft as a wedding chair. A huge cabinet to fit a wide-screen TV, the latest CD player and a tape deck with speakers blaring *blang-bleng-blang-bleng*. Also, notice the appliances stored behind glass—from food warmers to electric pots, toasters, stand mixers, juicers, hissing irons, fancy frying pans and who knows what else. All made in Malaysia.

There are no more rocky roads, dusty in the dry season and submerged under deep puddles of water in the rainy season. It would be embarrassing if visitors came, that's how they think. All the roads, from the entry archway to the exit gate, are straight and smooth, paved with asphalt—and not just the main roads, the small alleyways too, so that motorbikes can drive over them comfortably. After all, the best motorbikes have to be driven over the best roads. But that doesn't mean the old beat-up bikes that are driven to the fields and the forest should drive over bad roads either—maybe they won't get paved until later, but they must be smooth. Plans to build new roads are also underway because a few people are planning to buy coaches—I mean, cars.

In Cottonwood Grove, everything had changed except this: the people's attitude towards Mat Dawuk.

After almost sixteen years, Mat Dawuk reappeared in Cottonwood Grove. The kids clamoured to ask: who was he, where was he from, why was he here, what was he like. Their parents feigned indifference, but they immediately knew what had to be done. 'No, this is not a question of revenge,' they would insist. It was simply an old business that had not yet been settled. In order to settle it, the concerned parties gathered to deliberate what action should be taken. They decided to keep this meeting a secret, just so that they wouldn't stoke unrest among the people. So, if you all ask today whether that meeting took place, most people won't know because only certain people knew.

But, of course, I know. You all don't need to know *how* I know. The most important thing is that now I am telling you so you know too.

'Soon, it will be the fasting month. Cottonwood Grove must be in a peaceful state when Ramadan comes,' that's what Secretary Muksin, Ranger Hartoyo's brother-in-law, said to start that secret meeting, after opening it with greetings and an exhortation to give thanks to God for blessing them with the favours of faith and good health.

'Yes, I agree with Mr Secretary. My child is scared to go to the mosque. I don't want him to be so afraid of that man that he can't participate in evening prayers. We can't let that happen. The people can't be left unsettled for too long,' said Official Agus, Cottonwood Grove's newly elected Village Head. Only recently turned thirty, he was the youngest man there.

'And that's nothing, Mr Village Head. My grandson had a fit after seeing him at the mosque. He was vomiting and couldn't keep anything down. His mother and father had to go to the hospital, back and forth, because the community health centre couldn't do anything for him. This certainly can't continue,' added the local Head of Religion, also known as Modin, who was also new, I don't really remember his name.

'Must we ban him from the mosque? Would something like that be appropriate? At a time when our mosque is so sparsely attended for congregational prayer, should we be preventing *anyone* from entering?' That was a question from Badrun, the Head of the Mosque Management Committee, who was Inayatun's cousin.

Everyone could sympathize with this point. The mosque manager had been lamenting the decline in attendance at mosque congregational prayers for a long time now because most of the people of Cottonwood Grove had gone abroad. And people who came to the mosque could not just be asked to leave without a good reason. Even so, everyone knew that wasn't the most disturbing thing. The issue that had led them to gather that night, in secret, wasn't so simple, but apparently, everyone was waiting for someone else to bring it up.

Secretary Muksin finally broke the silence. 'Is the person we are talking about bothering us by going into the mosque? Enough, let's be honest, this is an issue of someone whose very appearance on the *street* is bothersome.'

'Bothersome?' Hanan, Foreman Har's brother-in-law and Woodsman Hasan's brother, finally exploded with his question: a question that was immediately followed by another: 'This is a person who has killed dozens of people, maybe even hundreds for all we know, and we are calling him "bothersome"?'

Secretary Muskin, who felt that the appropriate atmosphere for the deliberations had now been set, quickly chimed in. 'Yes, you're right. That's what I mean. This is about someone who could bash our children's skulls just by rapping them with his knuckles. We are here now, discussing someone who would pounce on us or our wives from behind and break our necks as easily as twisting a papaya from a branch. Imagine!'

'And, allegedly, he killed three of our people,' Official Agus joined in with confidence.

'Allegedly?' Hanan retorted, glowering at Agus. This young village head was his wife's cousin and the son of Harsih, who was Overseer Harjo's youngest daughter. Plus, they say Hanan had spent quite a bit of time raising his youngest grandchild to the rank of village head. 'My two little brothers dead, is that what you call "allegedly", 'Gus? One of them was your uncle!'

The young village head, of course, shrank back, to be chastised in front of those assembled.

'And don't try to overlook my child, Hanan,' Pak Imam, who had thus far been silent, finally spoke up.

'Ah yes, your daughter. Tell me how can you appear so calm, Pak Imam, sir,' Hanan asked.

'Do I have to froth at the mouth like a raving madman, 'Nan? If I did, would the bastard suddenly choke, collapse to the ground, and die? What's more, while I'm trying to be calm or at the very least pretending to be calm, I can think for a moment about how to finish that bastard once and for all.'

'Finish him? What do you mean?' Badrun, the mosque manager, didn't understand what his uncle was implying.

'Are we meeting tonight because we want to appoint him to the mosque management committee, 'Drun? Or, is there a tutor position that's open that we'd like to offer him, Secretary Muksin?' Pak Imam demanded.

'Yes, we should send him away as soon as possible,' Muksin responded.

'Where do you want to send him to?' Pak Imam snapped. 'To Deep Well Village, to Galeng Gede, off the island of Java, out of Indonesia or to the North Pole? I'm telling you, even if we throw him onto Jabalkat Mountain, as long as he is still breathing through that sunken nose of his, as long as he is still standing and walking on his crippled feet, that bastard will return to Cottonwood Grove.'

'If that's how it is, then we have to coordinate this with the responsible party,' Official Agus cut him off forcefully.

Pak Imam glared. 'Mr Village Head, sir, did you not participate in the attack on Mat Dawuk in front of the health centre?'

'Well, at that time I was still quite young, sir. So, no, I didn't participate,' he replied evenly.

'That figures.'

'So, what now? Should we contact the police chief straightaway? I have the number. If you want, I can call them right now.'

Pak Imam massaged his forehead. 'You don't have to go through all that trouble. It's better to call the Cottonwood Grove Civil Defence Commander. Please coordinate it however you can so that the police don't know about it since they don't need to bother with what will happen here.'

The young village head was confused.

Pak Imam looked toward Hanan, growing more agitated. 'Can you please explain this to your cousin, 'Nan? And don't forget to tell him how his grandfather was made into a lifelong couch potato by the grandfather of the bastard we are talking about.'

'It's like this, 'Gus.' Hanan was the only person in the room who called the young village head by his name. 'After being flattened and drenched in blood, like a fried catfish smeared with sambal, thrown into the back of the patrol truck like a wet sarong, completely limp, a week later, that bastard was roaming the streets of Cottonwood Grove. What could the police do?' Hanan ranted as if the police officers he was insulting were right before him.

'Well, in fact, what did they do?' Village Head Agus asked.

'They didn't do anything, and that's the problem!' Hanan snapped at his mild cousin. 'It should have been that with one stomp or one kick, they had finished him. But they let him be. I think they even let him go on purpose so that the bastard could get out of jail. And now, after years and years, he is still giving us trouble. What the hell use are they? Told to work on the record, they're incompetent, asked to work off the record, and they still can't take care of it!' Hanan's face was turning red.

'If you had been able to drag your cowardly little brother to court instead of helping him run off to Malaysia, then we wouldn't be in this situation, 'Nan,' Pak Imam huffed.

Hanan was surprised to hear that.

'You want to bring that up again, Pak Imam? Fine.' He rolled up his sleeves. 'If it wasn't for your loose daughter, would my little brother Foreman Har have died in such a terrible way?'

Pak Imam fell silent in response, making everyone present, about fourteen people, fall silent too.

'I lost two younger brothers, Pak Imam. Two brothers. And the rice cooked for the second one's funeral reception is still warm.'

There was no answer. Compared to the others, Hanan could be considered the one who had the most stake in this matter. Not long after his brother-in-law, Foreman Har, was killed in the fateful incident fourteen years ago, Woodsman Hasan died, falling from a building. Of course, it could be no other way, he was sure that Woodsman Hasan had been killed by the same man.

'It's best that we return to the issue at hand. And I must emphasize here that to face a threat like this, it's best to strengthen our unity and community.' Carik Kuksin once again became the mediator.

Softening the tone of his voice, as if he was realizing that there was no benefit in pursuing that matter, Pak Imam cleared his throat. 'So, what's your plan?' The question was for Hanan.

'And what is your plan?' Hanan asked in return.

'Enough, Hanan. I am trying to be agreeable. Don't just throw it back to me like that.' Pak Imam scowled again.

'You are older than I am. And you just said that you were trying to remain calm so that you could think of a way to handle this, isn't that right?'

'I'm a simple man: we finish him. We don't have to beat around the bush.'

'But don't we all know that finishing him is no simple matter?'

Pak Imam again massaged his brow. 'Right, that's why I just asked you what your plan was.'

So complicated. This, indeed, was no easy thing.

Inhaling tentatively, Hanan explained that he had asked help from his two gurus, that's what he called the men—a witchdoctor and a *kyai*, or maybe they both were witchdoctors, I don't know—that just recently he had asked for help in making Official Agus win the election for village head of Cottonwood Grove the previous year, with success. 'They have already said that they are willing,' he concluded.

'Can they do it?'

'You don't trust my gurus, Pak Imam?'

'I don't mean any harm, 'Nan. But this isn't a village head election. It's not just a matter of making someone's eyes blur over or moving their hand so that they vote for a certain candidate. We all already know—except for maybe your cousin here—the kind of creature we are facing.'

'If you don't have any faith in my gurus, maybe you can find us one who is more powerful.' Hanan's voice sounded a bit indignant, but he also appeared to be controlling himself, maybe so that the meeting would quickly reach a consensus.

'I was told by an acquaintance of mine that a *dukdeng* has some unfinished business with Dulawi. And after hearing that one of Dulawi's descendants was still alive and causing problems, he said he was willing to join us in facing him, without payment.'

'No matter how much payment he asked for, if he could take care of that rotten louse, I would help with the effort, Pak Imam,' Hanan said dismissively. 'But, more or less, what is the plan? What are we going to ask these men to do?'

'What is your plan?' Imam asked back, repeating the question that he had been asking Hanan since the beginning. 'Or maybe someone else has an idea?' He looked out at the others in attendance, who, this time, were listening more attentively.

'Let's try it!' Hanan replied, decisive and terse.

'And if we fail?'

'Didn't you just say that you had found a *dukdeng*? So

he's powerful, right? Even invincible, can't fail? Or you don't trust the man that you chose?'

'It's not that, 'Nan. You—we—already tried it when he was in prison, right? And failed. What if that happens again?'

'We'll find another way that's more effective. And then try again. If we've done that and it still doesn't work, well, I don't know. Once we've tried everything, all we can do is leave it up to God.'

The meeting that had started so energetically ended with the familiar uncertainty. But, whatever the case, the people of Cottonwood Grove, above all Pak Imam and Hanan, the two men who were the most invested, knew that this issue of Mat Dawuk absolutely could not wait. They had to move forward, no matter how rough the plans were. And it was with that same uncertainty they asked for help. People said that Pak Imam had to sell his land to hire his guy, while Hanan had to pawn his pickup truck to pay for the services of the men he had called his gurus.

And it turned out the result wasn't bad. I mean, they didn't really succeed, but neither did they totally fail. Those men they sent for didn't snuff out Mat Dawuk's soul all at once, but when Mat Dawuk came to the mosque to pray, he didn't look well. This is what gave the men a little more confidence. They suddenly felt reassured that Mat Dawuk could be defeated. In the end, they did something they had never planned to do, what I told you about that day: the assault. The pity—yes, the pity—is that you all didn't hear the whole story of what happened.

But you have nothing to worry about. Here I am.

A Waning Moon on Mid-Sha'ban

THE WANING MOON on the night of Mid-Sha'ban looked weak and old against the pitch black night sky, black like the last few drops of coffee stirred again with the grounds in the cup. Yes, like in my cup here.

On that night, when many ask God for forgiveness and pray for good fortune in the coming year, feet were advancing with assurance. Nervous but assured. From all eight directions of the wind, they came. Drawing closer, ever closer. Like hunters with their nets and weapons, their steps were slow and calculated, in synchrony. It had to be so—*had to*. Let there be no unplanned movement, no misstep, that might disrupt the mood of determination. They didn't want to fail again; they must not fail again. They had already tried it once, but in a mob attack, spontaneous, full of rage, out of control, which meant that there was work left to do, matters left to be settled that very night. It was infuriating and inconvenient. So, let that not happen again. It must not be repeated.

Tonight, everything had to be finished. The clamouring in their ears had to be silenced. The thorn in their flesh had to be pulled out and the wound cleaned. The dust in their eyes, that up until now had been smarting and blinding them, had to be rubbed away. The charcoal smeared across their face had to be washed off immediately. There was no other time. It had to be tonight.

But they knew that if they were hunters with nets, weapons and plans, their target there in the distance wasn't the kind of fawn that could be captured in a single ambush. He had already escaped death many times. Witchcraft, black magic, prison, it was as if none of them were a match for his soul. He was what we call *menter*—standing tall and proud, like the karst cliffs along Java's northern coast. They might look insignificant, but they hold their position as time passes, right at Tanjung Kodok beach on the edge of the Java Sea. He was the Daendel's Road: almost without beginning or end, foreboding and full of secrets.

They kept advancing, drawing together as they drew closer to the cow shed at the edge of the forest. They were a posse—unified in silence and in darkness.

Dark clouds hung low over the Cottonwood Grove forest and its village. The waning Mid-Sha'ban moon was weak and getting weaker, guarding what was left of its glow like an eyewitness who prefers to stay anonymous. The sounds of night insects were muted; perhaps they were the first living creatures—aside from the attackers, of course—who caught the smell of death hanging in the night air. It was overpowering. Maybe the rest were pretending not to notice. Only the wild dogs' weak, short, and mournful howls echoed faintly from the deep interior of the forest.

Ah, this is a pretty good introduction to a tragedy, isn't

it? Maybe I should stop re-reading Bastian Tito novels and start thinking about writing a book myself, of my own stories—do you have any connections to a publisher, brother?

Now, they were close enough to the shed house. A dim glow of lantern light came through the cracks in the bamboo walls. It was the only house in Cottonwood Grove left without electricity. As they crept closer, the attackers began to hear something coming from inside that much-whispered about house. Indian music, soft and sad, was being played as if being played for the last time.

'*Tere bina zindagi se koi...*' The smooth, majestic and melancholy voice seemed to tug on the listener from a distant past—from the singer, Kishore Kumar. Without you, this life means nothing; that's basically what the song from the old film was saying.

Even though it was melancholy, it didn't sound sad but rather gave the impression of being resigned to fate. In any case, the song put the attackers on alert. Even if one of Yoppie Latul's most frenzied *dangdut* songs had been playing, they would still have thought it best to be cautious. Because the song was coming from that shed.

That old cow shed on the edge of the forest...You all wouldn't be considered scaredy-cats if you shuddered just to look upon it from a distance, what's more on a dark night like that. Woodsman Hasan was the only person who had witnessed the killing—they believed it, and indeed it was so—but it was all too easy for the people of Cottonwood Grove to imagine how Inayatun had pressed her hand to the wound in her bulging stomach to no avail, gasping for air as the blood drained from her body and her head drooped forward, how Mat Dawuk had pulled out the bloody knife with eyes full of jealous rage. It wasn't hard to think of Foreman Har's shocked expression as the hatchet split his chest open, and his blood gushed out onto the dirt floor and spurted out onto his killer's ugly face. And the killer, that Grim Reaper, was now inside the cow shed they were headed for.

Before the man with the cleft lip suddenly reappeared and piqued the curiosity of all the children at the mosque, almost fifteen years had passed without the people of Cottonwood Grove hearing much about him. And since they had first cast him aside as a child, they had never really known what he did, it was all hearsay. Even so, they could easily imagine the rattle of his nunchucks as they smashed open a skull or shattered a pair of knees; they could practically hear the cracking of the bones broken by his big and terrifying hands.

And, of course, the image that still haunted those who came sneaking that dark night, was Mat Dawuk stained with blood, sunken chest, shattered arms and legs, an almost shapeless ruin, still living and breathing three days later. This man, who they were about to face, would have been frightening had he come out swinging but filled them with even more horror in this moment of stillness.

'*Zindagi nahi…zindagi nahi…zindagi nahi…*'

I can be sure that no one in the posse understood that the lyrics just before the end of the song were saying, 'There is no more life, no more life, no more life.' But, even without understanding, they knew that in a short time someone—whoever it would be—would lose their soul.

'*Tere bina zindagi se shikwa...to nahi.*'

Each word of the last line of that old song was drawn out before finally coming to an end. Then, complete silence.

Now, there were only four paces between the attackers and the bamboo wall of the shed. There were at least twenty-five people standing in a circle around it, like a fence enclosing a vegetable garden. Aside from the front door and the kitchen door in the back, the house had no other doors or windows. So, in front of the house, a dozen people stood thigh to thigh, exactly like men praying in congregation. About seven were waiting at the back door. The rest encircled the two sides of the house, standing evenly spaced. They were ready to spring into action should any sound or movement come from inside.

Then, 'Click!'

So my guess was correct; he was playing his songs on a battery-powered cassette tape. That was the sound of the play button popping back up after the cassette had reached its end. The dark prevented me from knowing more about what happened, but I suspect that sound must have startled a few people—there were some errant shuffling footsteps. If I had been the man inside that shed, I would have known that a large group of people surrounded my house. I wouldn't be surprised if the attackers were tightening their grip on the weapons in their hands.

Someone gave the sign for the attackers to stay calm and control themselves, they mustn't act carelessly, mustn't rush. If I could guess from his silhouette, I would say it was Pak Imam. He was among the dozen or so men standing in front of the house along with Hanan, Village Head Agus, Secretary Muksin, and a few others from Cottonwood Grove whose faces I couldn't quite make out. I am fairly certain there were two people I didn't know, although their faces were also obscured. They must have been the men Imam and Hanan had brought in to help.

One of the men in front of the house advanced a step. It was Pak Imam.

Imamudin, the father of Inayatun, that headstrong girl who everyone thought had been killed by her own husband, her hideous husband who he had never accepted as his son-in-law. He actually owned that cow shed at the edge of the forest and even in the dark, I could see that step—heavy and half hesitating—advancing with a forced courage, like an earnest kid being urged on by his friends.

'Mat!' he shouted, his voice shaking. 'Come out here!'

That call was answered only by his own exhalation. The forest and the night creatures and the twenty-four other men surrounding that house stayed silent and waited.

'Mat! I know you're inside, and I know you're not asleep!' He shouted again. 'We still have some business left! Let us finish it now!'

After taking a pause, with the tension palpably rising, Pak Imam shouted again—not an appeal, but a threat. His voice still shook from trepidation and resentment, but now he was starting to feel a little bit bold. 'All right then. Whether you come out or not, we will finish this!'

For the first time, he used the word 'we'. Of course, he must have said it to fortify his threat. But at the same time, he knew very well there was no way he could face his unacknowledged son-in-law alone. Even with his posse all around him, the man he called to still terrified him.

And again, a pause. This time, it felt longer and more strained. In the darkness, the attackers' eyes signalled to each other, sharing and upholding their code of caution and determined readiness.

Right then, there was some movement inside the shed. Then, a moment later, everyone could see the kerosene lamp inside the house move. The men held their breath, trying with all their might to calm their nerves, when slowly and calmly someone opened the door from the inside.

The figure they were hunting appeared in the doorway. It was Mat Dawuk, with the kerosene lamp in his hand. The flickering flame illuminated only part of his figure. The rest of his ugly face was shrouded in morphing, quivering shadows. He seemed to be in pain—so it was true; he was wounded. But that didn't prevent him from assuming a polite expression as soon as he realized who he was looking at.

'Ah, father. How unusual to see you here at this hour. Is everything all right?' greeted Mat Dawuk.

Pak Imam retorted coarsely and full of disgust. 'I'm not your father.'

Mat greeted that retort with the same polite face and a smile. 'Yes, but you are my wife's father.'

'My daughter is dead. And I never had a son-in-law like you.'

Mat smiled and nodded as if he had just heard some wise advice from a respected elder.

'*Monggo pinarak*. Please come in.' Mat used high Javanese to welcome his father-in-law, who would not acknowledge him. 'Welcome, please come in, *monggo, monggo*,' he repeated, inviting in all the others.

Of course, no one stepped forward. They just looked at each other.

'Mat!' Pak Imam's voice broke the silence. 'We're not here to talk. So let's get to it.'

'How do you mean, father?' Mat Dawuk was still using his most polite speech.

'Do you know what the people of Cottonwood Grove think of your return?'

Mat Dawuk shook his head. 'No, father. No one has spoken to me. I've heard the children talking amongst themselves, but no one spoke to me directly.'

'You're not wanted here. You should know that without having to be told.'

'What exactly are the people saying, if I might ask?'

'You disturb us.'

Mat nodded, trying to show that he understood. 'If that's the case, then, I sincerely apologize.'

'Sure, it's easy enough to apologize!' Pak Imam said, sounding fierce but shaky.

'So, father, according to you, what should I do?'

'According to you, what should someone who killed my daughter, Foreman Har, and Woodsman Hasan do, huh?'

The conversation had finally landed there. Mat Dawuk appeared to heave a breath, was quiet for a moment, and then hung the kerosene lamp on a small nail in the doorpost.

'I have killed people, it's true,' Mat said in a low voice, with audible regret. 'But father, you know, just as I have already told you, I didn't kill any one of the people that you just named. And just for you, father, let me say once more,' he drew in another breath, 'I did not kill Inayatun. I did not kill my wife.' Those were the most forceful words he had spoken up until that point. And from his cleft lip came a hiss.

'If all the scoundrels admitted to their crimes, the prisons would be full!' Pak Imam replied scornfully.

'That's true, father,' Mat Dawuk nodded again and then continued as if talking to himself, 'if all wrongdoers admitted to their crimes, then I certainly wouldn't have so many guests here tonight.' Of course, the men weren't stupid enough to miss the fact that his mumbled comment was for them to hear—for the one who had trafficked people to Malaysia; for the one who became village head because he had paid a conjurer and bought the election; for one who dabbled in black magic but wore the black *peci* hat of a haji. Their hands once again tightened their grip on their weapons.

They pressed their chattering teeth together and held their positions, though their feet were itching to advance in attack.

'Enough, Pak Imam!' Hanan, who stood two men away from the one he was addressing, interrupted. 'We're not here to have a Village Council meeting, are we?' He pulled out his machete, brandishing it. A few men tried to calm him down. Mat didn't look too concerned.

'What would Father and his entourage like me to do?'

he asked, returning to the previous conversation.

'Surrender voluntarily and confess to killing Woodsman Hasan before the police, and reaffirm that you killed Inayatun and Foreman Har, or…'

'Or?'

'We will force you, in any way we can, to surrender—meaning, we'll take care of this business without the police.'

Mat nodded yet again. A deep nod, as if truly considering the proposal. 'It's like this, Pak…' Mat's voice sounded like a young bachelor trying to persuade his parents to let him stay single longer. 'Let's say I agree, and then you all hand me over to the police, what's the point? I have already served my time for the death of my wife and Foreman Har. If that punishment was lighter than what you all hoped for, that wasn't my decision—and maybe it was because Woodsman Hasan disappeared right when he was supposed to give testimony. I'm a stupid man, illiterate, but I know I can't be tried twice for the same crime. Regarding Woodsman Hasan, I already told those involved that I wasn't the one who killed him. But if I did admit to it before the police, is there someone to serve as a witness?'

'So you want us to force you?' Pak Imam glowered.

'Why do you think you have to force me, Father?' Mat asked in return.

'What do you mean?'

'If you ask me nicely, I will surrender,' Mat said, cold and steady.

In the darkness, Pak Imam's face was visibly strained. He wasn't expecting that, and it made him wary. He took a step back, then solidified his fighting stance. That movement, no matter how small, put the men around him on guard. But after a few moments, when Mat made no further move, they just looked at one another.

'We still don't understand what you mean, Mat.'

'I came home to be closer to my wife—whatever you think about that, sir. If I am allowed to live, I want to visit her grave as often as I can. If I die, at least I will die close to her.'

As soon as he finished speaking, Mat put his hand into his tattered cargo pants pocket. He took out a dark coloured object, visible only in the light of the kerosene lantern hanging on the doorpost. When he opened his grasp, Pak Imam and the other attackers took a step backwards in shock, now ready to use their weapons. No doubt about it, in Mat's hand were the nunchucks—this was the first time any of these men were actually seeing that infamous object, rumoured to have split so many skulls and shattered so many kneecaps.

How was that weapon still with him? I don't know. Was it a new weapon? It didn't look like it—and why would he have gotten a new one when he had repeatedly said that he no longer had a purpose in life? The object didn't look that different from the one that I knew of, but if it was the same pair he had used to slaughter his victims, how had he been able to keep it with him? There's no way he could have brought it with him to prison without the guards discovering it. Had he left it in his house? If so, could it really have lain there, untouched, for the more than dozen years he had been away?

Only he himself could explain.

'Please take it,' Mat held out his hand, offering up his weapon.

Pak Imam leaned his body backwards, as if he were dodging a blow. The men with him tightened up their formation. All their weapons were now drawn, but no one rushed forward to start the attack.

As if he knew what his father-in-law and the men surrounding his house were thinking, Mat stooped to place the weapon in his hand on the ground—slowly and full of feeling. Under the melancholy flicker of the dim kerosene lamp, it was like a final goodbye to a friend. A soft, clear rattling sounded when the nunchuck's two sticks touched the ground and nudged some pebbles. The attackers were tense, transfixed, like little kids watching the climax fight scene between Barry Prima and Advent Bangun in a martial arts film from the eighties.

Mat Dawuk slowly stepped back, distancing himself from his weapon, lying in the dirt.

'Grab it!' Pak Imam gave the order. Someone stepped forward and picked up the nunchucks. The kerosene light falling across his face showed his alarmed expression. Neither of the fighting sticks was thicker than a thumb or longer than a man's middle finger. Fastened together with an iron chain no longer than nine inches, they looked like an ordinary toy, not two leaden objects that seemed to weigh five kilos each. The man was certain that Mat Dawuk had just surrendered his primary murder weapon.

But his father-in-law remained uncertain. 'Do you think we will believe your trickery so easily?' he sneered.

'Must I bind my wrists?' Mat burst out in reply.

'Take the amulet from around your neck!' Pak Imam ordered.

Mat Dawuk smiled in disbelief. 'This is just an ordinary necklace my grandfather gave me.' There was a tone of objection in his voice.

'Bullshit! Hasn't it kept you alive since the beating in front of the Galeng Gede Health Centre?'

'Father, you're pious and learned, a religious man. Are you telling me you still believe in things like that?'

'But I'm Javanese, Mat! And you are, too. Enough, don't try to fool me.'

Silent for a moment, Mat held up a finger. 'On one condition…'

Pak Imam, whose courage had swelled after seeing signs of Mat Dawuk's weakness, laughed. 'You want to bargain? We're not at the market, Mat.'

'If I cannot be with my grandfather in my last moments, at least allow me the opportunity to face God.'

'Don't worry, you'll be facing God very soon.' Pak Imam chuckled after he said that. Now he was sounding like a crafty, middling criminal in a television series.

'Take me to the mosque first. After that, it's up to all of you.'

Pak Imam and the men near him exchanged glances. Someone, one of the outsiders who had been asked for help, nodded. 'Fine. Take off that necklace immediately.'

Moving slowly, Mat undid the two highest buttons on his shirt, moved his hand around under the fabric, and then kissed something in his hand. Pausing momentarily, as if lost in thought, he slipped the simple cord necklace from his neck. From the necklace hung a pouch made by his grandfather, Mbah Dulawi, who had given it to Mat along with his name. It contained a small scroll amulet with a few holy verses written on it—that's what I know. The people of Cottonwood Grove, including that wretched in-law, must have believed that half of Mat Dawuk's soul was held in that pouch.

Mat Dawuk held the necklace out to Pak Imam. 'If you don't want to keep it, father, I beg you to bury it with me.'

This time, Pak Imam took it. His hand was trembling, and not from the cold night air. He showed it to the men to either side of him before handing it over and nodding in confirmation.

'Now, tell us your weakness.' Pak Imam was like a haughty prayer recitation teacher testing his students.

Mat Dawuk smiled again out into the night. This old man wants everything clean, maybe that's what he was thinking. Seeming to consider this for a moment, he smiled again, the smile of a compliant, ugly, son-in-law. Then, he said: 'Your daughter.'

This was met with a furious snort.

'Inayatun has already taken all my power.'

Pak Imam spat. 'You're trying to soften my heart with some cheesy Melayu song lyrics? Bah!'

Mat stepped back from where he had been standing. He took the kerosene lamp from its hook with his right hand while his left hand undid the rest of the buttons of his shirt. He then moved the lantern closer to his chest, which was now fully exposed. It wasn't as clear as it would have been in broad daylight, but everyone could see that, at one time, he had been gravely injured; his ribs had been broken and worse. But he didn't seem to be displaying all that, instead revealing a large scar on the left side of his torso.

'This must be familiar to one of you, right?' Mat, this time, was quite clearly in pain.

Pak Imam looked toward the man next to him, not seeming to understand that Mat Dawuk was showing him his own handiwork.

'How do we know you're not faking, Mat?'

Ah, that man was truly belligerent. No wonder his child grew up to be a headstrong and contrary young woman.

Mat shook his head. He moved the kerosene lamp from his right hand to his left.

The attackers, already on edge, gasped when Mat slammed his right hand without warning into the nail on the door post that had been serving as the lantern hook. The shed, which was surrounded, shook. Trembling for a moment, letting out a small groan, Mat opened his palm, moving his other hand closer to shine a light on it. Blood was dripping out, looking darker than it should have in the phosphorescent lantern light.

'I have nothing left to prevent you all from killing me. So it's whenever you are ready.' He reached out to place the lantern back on its hook.

But before the lamp was correctly settled, a dark form hurtled in his direction. A hard and furious lunge struck Mat Dawuk's thigh, and he was hurled sideways against the door to his house. The lantern was knocked from his hand

and clattered down to the ground as his body collapsed. Clearly, he was no longer as strong as he once had been. In the quivering lantern light, Mat Dawuk clutched at his head, which looked to have struck the doorframe, holding back a cry of pain. When he tried to get up, a hard kick from another foot met his chin, snapping his head back, this time drooping weakly to the ground.

'Hit him! Tie him up!' a voice ordered.

Another man leapt forward with a rubber cord as thick as a thumb in his hand, as if it all was going just as they had planned. As Mat staggered and tried to stand, the hand he should have used to support his body was bound behind his back, with a twist of rope that connected to the noose that was already around his neck. Then, as he tried again to stand, a kick knocked both feet out from under him. With wrists bound, he was helpless to stop his fall. Mat Dawuk must have understood what he was about to undergo.

'Sir, I beg you, take me to the mosque first,' Mat Dawuk said weakly. 'You promised you would.' But a foot landed squarely on his stomach in reply.

Pak Imam, the father-in-law who now looked even more cocksure, haughtily said: 'So that you can look like Mat Modar and die feeling like a hero, is that it?' Another kick, this time to Mat's back, accompanied Pak Imam's words. 'Do you think we're stupid?

I could no longer see Mat Dawuk's face from my hiding place. All I could see was his hands and feet, still struggling against the rope that bound them.

There were the sickening thuds of three or four more

kicks and blows. 'Drag him inside!' Pak Imam commanded again.

'Why don't we finish him first?' Hanan's voice boomed.

'It's enough, we don't have to wear ourselves out.'

And a few people yanked sharply on the rope, tautening the noose and forcing Mat's face to look up at them. They dragged his large body through the doorway into the shed. Now I could see his face again. His eyes were bulging out, certainly because he was being choked, but perhaps also with rage at his father-in-law's broken promise. A few other men went in.

Three or four more blows were heard.

'Tie him up on the bed,' Pak Imam said. 'Tie him up tightly.'

Someone else said, 'Gag him. If he cries out, the whole village will hear. The police will find out.'

Not long after, the attackers came out of that shed—the house where Inayatun and Foreman Har had met their end and where Mat Dawuk might soon meet his. Pak Imam, the true owner of the house, came out last. Walking backwards, he closed the door and locked it from the outside. Still walking backwards, he grabbed the kerosene lantern from its hook, removed the glass cover to expose the flame, loosened the cap to the porcelain tank, and now having what he considered to be the right distance, threw the lantern onto the thatched roof. It was a good throw. The lantern traced a graceful arc of light in the dark sky before alighting perfectly on the spilt oil and almost instantaneously bursting into a flame that quickly spread. The whole house was soon blazing brightly.

The fire surged, swallowing the thatch roof that hadn't been replaced for decades and devouring the rotted wooden battens. The attackers looked on with satisfaction and perhaps also with a bit of amazement that the accursed creature who had haunted them for decades could be taken care of so easily. It turned out the pest that had plagued them could be exterminated. They must have truly enjoyed every lick of flame destroying that cursed shed, waiting impatiently for the fire to melt all the flesh off Mat Dawuk's wrecked body so that they could hear his bones crack and his skull explode. His ugly face would disappear, and then it would be forgotten. The children wouldn't ask about him anymore. And nothing would be left of that rotten louse that had ruined their sound sleep for decades except dust. Dust.

In my hiding place, I began to curse myself for being there, witnessing that whole hellish incident but doing nothing.

Then came the jarring sound.

'*Hghg ghgh ghghgh hg hghg…hghghg…hg hghg…hghghg hghg…hghg…hghg…hghg…hghg hg…*' That's all I heard. It was the discordant sound of a song being sung through his nose—his broken nose—or, more precisely, his broken nose and his gagged mouth. But everyone there, waiting for their biggest enemy to be scorched down into a lump of coal, recognized the tune as that of the old song that had been playing when they arrived.

One of the attackers, it looked like Hanan, cursed violently and tried to rush inside. But a few others held him back, as the flames pounced on the bamboo walls, and the three posts that supported the veranda's roof became pillars of fire. 'Don't dirty your hands, 'Nan. Those are just the groans of a dying sinner,' Pak Imam counselled.

'*Hghghg hghg...hghghg hghg...hghghg hghg...*'

The sound coming from Mat Dawuk's nose was so unpleasant, so upsetting; if someone was singing like that right in front of you, you would punch him in the face. But, somehow, it was even more poignant than the original song because it wasn't really coming from his nose but his heart. I'm not kidding! Ah, more precisely, it was coming from the heart of a man who knew he was about to die—so serene in the face of impending sorrow. It was like the last, gasped words from a film hero, when the viewer believes that he should already be dead. Maybe we're not sure whether he will live, but those stammered words make us feel we have the right to hope that he will survive, that he will live and be happy.

'*Hghghg hghg...hghghg hghg...hghghg hghg...*'

Then, a bizarre thing happened. I saw one of the attackers, who was standing on the outermost ranks, suddenly fall to the ground, first down to a crumpled seat and then collapse flat onto the ground. The people around him were confused. But, before they understood what had happened, someone on the other side fell headlong, and then rolled over onto his side. The attackers grew nervous. Then another fell—first he was standing, then he was flat on his face.

'Watch out, this is *sirep* magic! He's putting us all to sleep!' I heard Pak Imam say just before he stumbled backwards and collapsed. Then another man followed and another.

My own head suddenly felt heavy. The dark sky, reddish from the burning shed, seemed to turn grey and then totally white. As I shook my head again and again, as strongly as I could, forcing my eyelids open, I realized what was happening. Whatever black magic had struck the posse of attackers was getting me, too.

Was this overpowering fatigue caused by the discordant rhythm coming out of Mat Dawuk's nose? I wasn't sure. From the beginning he looked as though he had no intention of fighting back. What's more…this magic was very powerful. I hadn't seen Mat for a long time and didn't know much about what had happened to him. But…as strong as this? No. This wasn't him. This *sirep* magic was coming from someone else, someone more powerful.

I gave my head another forceful shake, trying to hold it up as it was forced to bow forward. But, no, there was nothing I could do. As soon as my head was again overpowered by fatigue, my body was blanketed in an incredible sense of exhaustion and then bewilderment. I knew this power could only be wielded by someone very skilled. I couldn't fight it—I didn't think anyone could. But, before I truly fell, I was struck by a fierce wind. Then, a flash of a figure, a shadow or something like that, circled around the shed, encircled the attackers and forced its way in. And then…

And then…that's it. I don't know what happened next.

Where Did Warto Kemplung Go?

'A FIRE DESTROYED a cow shed near the forest on the outskirts of Cottonwood Grove Village, Friday (5/6). The location, far from the centre of town, did not allow for rescue attempts. According to eyewitnesses, the fire occurred in the middle of the night, with uncertain cause. Yasir, a Village Administrator from Cottonwood Grove, said there were no human casualties in the incident. Only one calf was reported dead in the fire. The loss is estimated to be about twelve million rupiah.'

I smiled sourly as I read that short article, which was given the title of only 'Cottonwood Grove'—which, of course, wasn't really a title, just the place of incident. How unimportant the information that was recounted! And how poorly the news had been written! A new intern had worked on it, and even though it had been edited—and, unfortunately, I was the one who edited it—the short article was still terrible. It was included in the small section called 'The LoDowns' (a play on 'local town news') in the corner of a regional page that was mostly filled with classified ads and trifling updates on the activities of officials and sub-district level government agencies, other even less important news and inconsequential items so that our small newspaper could stay connected to even the most common reader (or at least that's what my managing editor said), but I was sure that no one read it. Even I, as its editor, would hardly have remembered the piece if Warto Kemplung hadn't told the story about Mat Dawuk the day after it was published. The article seemed even more pathetic when compared to the retelling of Warto Kemplung's story, which I had been working on for the past three days—without permission.

The people didn't call him Warto the Bullshitter for nothing—poring over a few parts of his story, I reminded myself that, of course, I couldn't just swallow everything he said, hook, line and sinker. But whoever read my re-telling later would have to agree he was quite a clever storyteller.

From his exaggerated style, which laid it on thick, the nickname *kemplung* was founded. He also sometimes identified too strongly with the characters he was talking about. (Although it must be emphasized here, his depiction of storytelling and its relationship to the deer and the tiger was apt: you don't need to ask the deer how it feels about tigers to tell a story about how it felt or what it did when it met one; a good storyteller should undoubtedly be able to imagine it.) But how did he seem to have been present at each incident? He seemed to assert, at least in certain parts of the story, that he had been there, had been part of it. Was he in fact Mbah Dulawi?

His storytelling style, which was so 'oral', was also difficult to transfer onto the page. There was no choice; I was forced to fiddle with it: take out sentences that had been spoken verbatim from their quotation marks because they worked better narrated, or, the opposite, put in quotation marks to create direct dialogue that would have been better as narration. I also had to reign in his blabbermouth, which sometimes got so worked up that it carried him away from his own story, even though in many parts I kept these asides intact so that readers would understand that someone had told the story to me. Ah, of course, I haven't yet mentioned the most exhausting thing: translating the story, which was told in Javanese except for the words borrowed from Malaysian and the lyrics of the Indian songs, into Bahasa Indonesia.

'Coffee, brother?' Bu Siti, the *warung* owner, was suddenly behind me.

I gave a small nod, realizing I had been sitting at the table in her café for at least fifteen minutes and hadn't ordered anything. 'Please don't make it too strong, Bu.'

Three minutes later, she returned with an overflowing cup in her hand. She set the coffee down politely but without giving me any special treatment, like most *warung* owners towards their regulars. How different from the hostile and grumpy way she had served Warto Kemplung. She was turning to go back into the kitchen when I stopped her with a question: 'Pak Warto isn't here, Bu?'

She turned her body hesitantly. 'Does he owe you some money?'

I shook my head.

She gave a small smile. 'Oh, I know. That bigmouth's idle claims must have taken you in.'

I blushed like a kid caught red-handed stealing a

mango from a neighbour's garden. Trying to find the right explanation, I finally fixed on a silly reply. 'It's not just me—even Anwar Ibrahim fell for it!'

'You believe that story about Anwar, brother?'

I shrugged. I had no answer. Defeated, I just scratched my head and said the only thing I could think of. 'At least, he's entertaining.'

The woman, about my mother's age, looked around the small coffee stall, with its three long tables and one wide bamboo divan. Aside from me, there were only four other people there—one pair playing chess, sitting at a table with two teenagers sharing games and music on their cellphones. They all already had their coffee. Maybe because there were no more customers who needed to be served, Bu Siti didn't walk away and sat down at the table across from me.

'Yes, Warto has always been like that. For as long as I can remember, he never seemed to have any money. And if he was feeling too embarrassed to put anything else on his unpaid tab, he would shoot his mouth off here and there so that people would give him coffee and cigarettes,' she said. I wanted to interrupt, but she didn't give me the chance, quickly continuing, 'But he's a good person.'

I nodded. I agreed with her, but I was also wondering about what else she might know. She fell silent, and as I was waiting for the right moment to ask who Warto Kemplung really was, she opened her mouth again. 'It used to be...'

And a moment later I was in the middle of her story about a smart and quiet young orphan named Anwar Tohari, the son of a poor woodcutter who had been beaten and humiliated by a forest overseer. Anwar forced himself to go to school when other kids his age chose to chop down trees, or become goatherds in neighbouring villages or work as lackeys in the limestone kiln in the village across the forest. Out of all the kids accepted into Mbah Dulawi's prayer house, he was one of only two chosen to also train in martial arts and supernatural self-defence. In the picture Bu Siti drew, this young man was 'fairly good-looking, a little bit like the singer S. Achmadi from the duo Awara.' Once he reached puberty, his guru and community put their hopes on his skill at prayer recitation, his earnest pursuit of knowledge, and his mystical abilities until the tragic love triangle that changed everything.

Anwar loved Rukaniyati, or Yati, and asked Mbah Dulawi to propose. Mbah Dulawi did indeed ask for Yati's hand, but not for Anwar—for Mahfud, Anwar's fellow student who also happened to be Dulawi's only son, the headstrong youth who, thanks to his recklessness, narrowly escaped being labelled a communist and suffering the consequences. When Anwar contested his guru's decision, Mbah Dulawi said, 'You have the right to better. But this is for everyone's greater good and happiness.' But it didn't turn out the way Mbah Dulawi hoped—nothing got any better after that decision, no one got anything better than they already had, and nobody ended up happy.

Mahfud, who at first thought that he had been favoured and rewarded by his father, discovered that Yati didn't love him. He then decided he was cursed and became convinced his wife hadn't been pure when he married her. Meanwhile, Anwar was broken-hearted and left Mbah Dulawi's prayer house. He went wandering off somewhere, until a few years later—so they say—he became known by the name Warto, a petty criminal who worked the bus terminals between Semarang and Jogjakarta, from Weri to Wonogiri. Yati died a painful death in childbirth, delivering a baby boy whose face didn't look like anyone—not his mother, not his father, not even the man suspected of being his father. Mbah Dulawi was wracked with guilt over his terrible mistake, and when he realized he would never be able to control Mahfud's unseemly behaviour, which had only gotten worse after Yati's death, he disappeared into the forest and never was seen again.

Anwar, who had now become Warto, reappeared after the crazy 'Petrus' era of mysterious killings came to an end—Bu Siti called it '*jaman wong dikarungi*', the time when people were stuffed into sacks. Once it seemed that alleged criminals and small-time toughs like him were no longer targeted, their bodies no longer stuffed into sacks or left rotting on the roadside, he returned home, but the people Warto was most hoping to see again were nowhere to be found. His guru had disappeared into the forest, the woman he loved had died giving birth to a child whose father refused to accept him, and on top of that his former fellow student, the man he considered to have taken the love that was rightfully his, had fallen too deeply into a broken life and died.

All he found was an ugly, neglected kid who had nobody. He spent a few aimless years and then left for Malaysia looking for work. When he returned from Malaysia he married a widow with two children, but it was plain to see theirs was not a happy home. He went back and forth to Malaysia for a while, but he must have been a failed pilgrim, unable to find work. And after he gave up on going back to Malaysia, Anwar Tohari, who had once been a promising young man with a face like S. Achmadi, now was no other than Warto Kemplung, Warto the Bullshitter.

'And what about you?' I blurted out.

The coffee seller looked embarrassed. Then, with a wistful smile she said, 'I was the neighbour girl who Mbah Dulawi intended to marry to his broken-hearted student. But he was never interested in me.'

'You mean that man…who was the S. Achmadi lookalike?'

She turned away. She didn't say anything, just bit her lower lip, but I could still see the lingering traces of her youthful beauty in that countenance.

She changed the subject. 'Drink your coffee, brother. It won't taste good once it's cold.'

'May I ask where Pak Warto lives…I mean, Pak Anwar?'

She gave an approximate location but hurriedly told me, 'But I don't think he's there.'

When my face showed curiosity, she continued, 'Last night, people are saying two detectives came and picked him up. I don't know exactly what the trouble was, but I heard it's because he knows something about a man from Cottonwood Grove named Imamudin, who disappeared five days ago.'

Bu Siti returned to her kitchen, leaving me stunned.

I drank my coffee in silence, like a man hypnotized. The cup still held its warmth, but my tongue tasted nothing. My eyes were glued to the inconsequential and poorly written news item about that burned cow shed. I shuddered, imagining the 'calf' that had perished inside it. It still wasn't clear how to connect the disappearance of Pak Imam and the shed fire to the whole story about Mat Dawuk, but I suddenly remembered how Warto Kemplung's feet had been covered in ash the morning he had made his indignant entrance at the coffee stall.

'I'm Mat'

ALMOST THE WHOLE fasting month, as I continued my routine work, I tried to uncover Warto Kemplung's whereabouts. A few times I visited the house, said to be his, but it was always shuttered, and as time passed, I gathered it was no longer occupied.

Meanwhile, I contacted at least five local police departments and three national police bureaus. I spoke to two Police Chiefs directly. But I didn't get one speck of information. Warto Kemplung, alias Anwar Tohari, had disappeared, and his whereabouts remained unknown, as if he had vanished into the heavens. After I started asking around, Bu Siti began bothering me with her questions and worries. None of the people in her *warung* or regulars who frequented other nearby coffee stalls knew anything. Maybe, since they found him so annoying, none of them cared.

The people in Cottonwood Grove also knew very little about the disappearance of Pak Imam. After a month had passed and there was still no word of him, they considered it possible he was dead—even so, his family told me they were still searching. Strangely, they didn't know anything about Warto Kemplung and just shook their heads when asked about Mat Dawuk. Everyone else in Cottonwood Grove did the same. No one knew—or at least seemed to know—any more about Warto Kemplung than what I knew. Even the one or two local busybodies couldn't say much more than, 'The Warto who hangs around that coffee stall, right? The one who likes to mooch cigarettes?' Of course, that didn't help at all.

Maybe because I had become so consumed by Warto Kemplung's story, I felt the people of Cottonwood Grove were hiding something from me. But, at the same time, no one seemed to act uncomfortable—or even care at all—when I tried to visit the alleged scene of the crime, the 'cow shed that burned down'. When I asked people about its location, they told me casually. No one warned me or tried to put me off, directly or indirectly. But most amazing was the fact that the place—a heap of rubble and ash, which, according to Warto Kemplung, was where Inayatun and Foreman Har were murdered about twenty years ago, where the people of Cottonwood Grove tried for the umpteenth time to obliterate Mat Dawuk, and the place I had imagined as holding the mystery of Pak Imam's disappearance—hadn't even been surrounded by police tape.

But honestly, why would the police cordon off a place that seemed to be nothing more than the site of a burned down old cow shed?

Fine. It seemed as though the whole world was conspiring to turn its back on me, leaving my questions to turn into a crashing confusion as all my theories and suspicions collided into one another. But I had already determined that I could not keep what Warto Kemplung had told me to myself. This story had to be shared.

One small problem now remained: there was no way I could tell Warto Kemplung's story as news, especially since I couldn't check doubtful facts or dubious sources. I would certainly meet with no success if I reached out to confirm the names of the people mentioned in the story, at least not the ones I would be able to contact because they were still alive. It was clear who they were—like the village administrators who participated in the secret meeting or the men who participated in the ambush. Unwilling and unable to force it into the form of straight journalism, after some consideration, remembering the creative writing that I had studied back on campus, I decided to adapt the story into a work of fiction.

Of course, before that, I had to fiddle with it; fix the syntax, re-check the usage of quotation marks, separate it into paragraphs, and shape it into a narrative frame that I hoped would be easier to read. I aligned the historical facts of the story, at least the parts about the Java forest and the people's resistance during the colonial era through the war for independence, with the history books I could find to minimize the possibility of anachronisms, but at the same time I had to maintain the sense that this story was being told by a huckster. It took a little additional work to clarify, explain or change the special phrases, the distinctive dialect and the idioms that would be too local or too strange for readers who weren't from around here.

At first, I weighed whether those explanations would be better as footnotes or placed at the end of the story. Still, after I thought about it, taking into account what would be the easiest and least disruptive for readers, I decided to place such explanation inside the body of the narration—for myself, I don't like it when pieces of prose or poetry are given footnotes.

I convinced my culture editor to eliminate the bad poetry written by civil servants seeking recognition and the chicken scratches of Parliament members that almost certainly had been written by their staff. Instead, it would be better to publish this story as a serial; that's what I advised. 'Boss, let us return to the old lost tradition when small newspapers published serials with pride,' I said (a bit over-dramatically, perhaps, in my attempts to convince him). Maybe because he took pity on me, the first instalment appeared in our newspaper a few days after Eid Al-Adha, and was to be published once a week, every Sunday. But, of course, it was published with the editor's caveat: 'Don't get your hopes up. If there's a good response, we'll continue. If not, be prepared to go back to editing bad poetry and chicken scratches.'

I titled the story 'A Dark Tale from Cottonwood Grove' and it appeared every Monday. After we ran the fourth instalment, my editor said that the response was pretty good. 'The readers feel like your story is depicting events that are close to their lives,' he said. Because of that, he was trying to get the story instalments published every day, as a proper serial should be. To do this, he asked me to make the story longer, or maybe make up a new story, or if it could be done, find a new writer who had access to a similar character so that there would be a stock of available stories if and when this serial of mine came to an end.

I was happy with this development and had begun to daydream about how compelling it would be to 'continue' what Warto Kemplung had already 'given' me when the following incident made me reconsider.

One morning, on the veranda of my rented house, I was re-reading the fourth instalment of the serial—regretting the choice of illustration to the right of the column, which I felt didn't fit, still finding a few typos, and punctuation marks that weren't right, and descriptions that could be too easily associated with someone's name or a certain place. I also felt that I, not the original teller of this tale, had gone too far with diction that was too elevated and overboard to represent the storytelling style of a loudmouth at a coffee stall who had once been a bus terminal thug and an illegal migrant worker in Malaysia. This had to be fixed.

As I entered my room to get a ballpoint pen to make notes and corrections, I heard a motorbike enter the front yard. When I returned to my seat and my newspaper, I found a man in dark and expensive-looking Levis, white Mizuno shoes with thick heels, a blue Polo T-shirt and a dark brown leather jacket with the zipper half-open, getting off his GL Pro. As he removed his helmet, the sunglasses perched on his nose momentarily caught the light, reflecting a rainbow. He came up onto the veranda confidently, almost arrogantly, and without asking for permission sat in the empty chair next to my table.

'Mustofa Abdul Wahab?' he asked, pushing his sunglasses up his head. I caught a whiff of his hair gel.

'Yeah, I'm Mustofa,' I replied, sneaking a glance at his face. He had dark brown skin, a square jaw, complete with a large and noticeable scar on his left cheekbone. Even so, I thought it wouldn't surprise me if a woman called him handsome.

He took something out from inside his jacket. It was our newspaper. He placed it on the table, folded open to the culture page—more precisely, to the serial that I had written.

'Pak Warto is full of shit. It would be better for everyone if your newspaper stopped running this garbage story,' he ordered. He tapped the author's name printed underneath the illustration—my name—with an object in his hand. At first, I thought it was a motorbike keychain. But after I got a good look, I could see it was a hefty switchblade. Make no mistake.

I froze, even as he stood and headed for his motorbike. 'And who are you?' I asked evenly.

'I'm Mat. Mat Dawuk.' He answered curtly, kickstarting the engine and rolling the throttle.

Hearing that name, I swallowed a chuckle. What a faker! He was clearly trying to intimidate me. Too bad—apparently, no one had told him that white Mizuno shoes, gelled hair, and a switchblade made a ludicrous combination for someone trying to come across as a thug. And he'd bought a newspaper! Since when could Mat Dawuk read?

Once the man was gone, it suddenly hit me that I had never even met Mat Dawuk, let alone had the chance to get to know him. I had never seen his ugly face for myself, his long, dried and matted hair, his black singlet tank, his cargo pants with oversized pockets, or his small but terrifying nunchucks. As a reporter, I should have maintained a healthy scepticism regarding whether a person named Mat Dawuk existed or was just a fiction. But I believed he did exist—yet, at the same time, I could not possibly believe all the tales Warto Kemplung had told.

I leaned back into my chair. My body suddenly felt weak, and my knees trembled.

As I thought of all the names Warto Kemplung had mentioned—the characters' strange histories, the lyrics to the Indian songs he had sung, and the ones I had copied down without certainty—I was overwhelmed by a flood of questions.

Who was dead? Who had disappeared? Who killed who?

Acknowledgements

EVER SINCE I watched *Machete* (2010), I have dreamed of telling the story of a migrant worker named Mat. After seven years, I told the story of a completely different Mat from the one in the film, but this in no way minimizes my debt to the story created by the director Robert Rodriguez. I needed so much time to develop this Mat's story, which is quite short, because for years I had so many Mats in my head but still didn't know whose story to tell or what kind of story to tell about him until a friend of mine, Irfan Afifi, told me about a man attacked by a mob because he was suspected of murdering his wife. Without Irfan's story, I would have never been able to begin the story of my Mat. And without the stories of other Indonesians, especially my close friends Abdhul Wahab and Erif Hadi Siswanto aka Hendro, who shared many of the dark (and bright) aspects of the life of migrant workers in Malaysia, and other conversations about Indian films and songs, it's quite possible I never would have written this story.

Every page in this book is dedicated to Qowim Mustofa, my coffee drinking companion who began his journey to Malaysia after this story was written. There is no doubt about it, he is my Warto Kemplung, our Warto Kemplung.

ALSO IN SPEAKING TIGER INTERNATIONAL FICTION

BEAUTY IS A WOUND

Eka Kurniawan

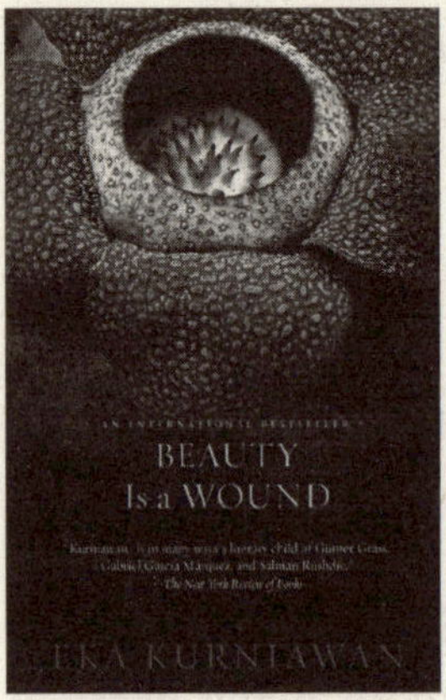

ISBN: 978-93-85755-68-2

Described as '*One Hundred Years of Solitude* kicked into another gear', *Beauty Is a Wound* combines history, satire, family tragedy, legend, humour and romance in a sweeping polyphony. The novel begins with the Japanese occupation of Indonesia, then a Dutch colony, during World War II. Dewi Ayu, a beautiful half-Dutch, half-Indonesian girl, is captured by Japanese soldiers along with twenty others and brutalized. After the US Army frees Indonesia—and Dewi—from the Japanese, Dewi finds her family untraceable and their mansion occupied by American soldiers. Struggling to survive, she turns to prostitution and soon becomes the most sought after prostitute in the land.

Dewi Ayu gives birth to three daughters, each as stunning as herself. Over the course of their lives, Dewi and her daughters are beset by incest, murder, bestiality, rape, insanity, monstrosity, and the often vengeful undead. However it is Dewi's fourth daughter—named Beauty in a cruelly inverted joke—who draws them all together and brings this epic tale to its final conclusion.

Drawing on local sources—folk tales and all-night shadow-puppet plays, with their bawdy wit and epic scope—Kurniawan's gleefully grotesque hyperbole functions as a scathing critique of his nation's troubled past: the rapacious offhand greed of colonialism; the chaotic struggle for independence; and the mass murders of perhaps a million 'Communists' in 1965, followed by three decades of Suharto's despotic rule. Kurniawan's distinctive voice brings something luscious yet astringent to contemporary literature.